the grump next door

EFFIE RAYE

Copyright © 2025 by Effie Raye

All rights reserved.

No part of this book may be reproduced in any form or by any electronic or mechanical means, including information storage and retrieval systems, without written permission from the author, except for the use of brief quotations in a book review.

Art - Searland Art

Cover - Effie Raye

If you want a gardener with rough hands and a cheeky smile to plough you under the mistletoe... Henry is your man.

Sweet, charming and with golden retriever energy, you might mistake him for a softie, but this puppy-eyed MMC ***bites.***

one

> OTTERLEIGH BAY VILLAGE NEWS
>
> Out with the old, in with the new.
> Mind the clipboards!

AMANDA

M Y SUITCASE LAY ON THE BED LIKE A GAPING MOUTH. Clothes spilt from its sides, an assortment of colours and fabrics, as I attempted to plan my days ahead. Taking the Christmas event booking had been a hot debate amongst my extended family, but the wealthy clients paid very well, and dealing with their nonsense had to be better than dealing with my family's.

'You're actually going then?' Megan asked from the doorway. She wore one of my hoodies, having stolen it like the feral little raccoon she was. Ever since she'd moved to Edinburgh and taken up residence in my spare room, my wardrobe had morphed into an unofficial charity shop for her. 'You're really working through Christmas?'

'Can you blame me? It's not like Mum and Dad aim for a Christmas movie-style celebration. Or celebrations,' I said, rolling a black jumper up and sliding it next to the other perfect fabric rolls in my case.

'Mum's going to be so mad.' Megan strode in and perched on the dressing table stool, sloshing some coffee onto her joggers as she sat. 'And Dad will do that thing where he pretends not to care, but blame Mum for it until we beg him to change the subject.'

'Maybe they'll learn to stop pulling us at both ends like we're Christmas crackers between petulant children. It's been years. I'm done being the puppet in between their arguments.' I placed a sweater dress beside the jumper, another neat little soldier lined up amongst the rest. Clothes that cost far more than I enjoyed spending, but that screamed I belonged amongst my clients.

Even if I didn't, really.

But half of the job was wrangling millionaires into believing that their money really does buy happiness, and the other half was looking like I deserved my rather hefty paycheque.

My Edinburgh flat tried its best to look festive despite my complete lack of decor. I'd spent enough Christmases believing in the magic and spirit of the season only to be surrounded by anger and resentment, before my parents' divorce, and after it.

I couldn't be more done with the whole bloody thing.

But my lack of festive cheer was thwarted the moment you stepped into the external hall. The building's committee strapped twinkly lights just about anywhere they could be affixed, and a matching wreath on every single door. The corridor looked like a party of elves had vomited all over the place.

And against Megan's best attempts to sneak in sparkly stuff whenever I went out, I kept the inside clinical. Candles. A plant that always looked a little worse for wear due to my stints away working, and Megan's lack of watering capabilities.

Megan lifted her eyebrows at me.

'But you *are* doing Christmas, just not with me,' she pouted, as had swooped in like the Grinch and swept her celebration into a sack.

'I'm coordinating it, not having fun without you, I promise. It's going to be long days arguing with suppliers and cleaning up messes, all while slapping a smile on my face,' I corrected, sliding my shoes into protective bags.

Megan snorted. 'Sounds like being back home.'

'But without the emotions. Other people's messy lives are much easier to deal with than mine.'

'You hate Christmas, how on earth can you be in charge of someone else's festive cheer?' She rifled through the bottles of perfume on my dressing table before spraying her wrist with one of them.

'I do.' I pulled on a boot. 'And it's much easier to deal with when it pays for several months' rent. Isn't that growth?'

'Bayview Manor.' Megan tasted the words, like they were slightly sour. 'Otterleigh Bay. Ten days. Millionaire family. Do they know you're a Scrooge in heels?'

'They know I'm an event planner who can conjure ice rinks out of car parks and reindeer out of thin air.' I pointed at my laptop, which sat open and bursting with spreadsheets and digital notes. 'They demanded "authentic Scottish festive magic." And sent a mood board with a stag in a scarf. *A scarf, Megan.* I'm saving them from themselves.'

She buried a smile in her mug. 'No, you're hiding.'

'There it is.'

Megan forever came in the guise of help or

support, but would use that soft voice of hers to chide me into relenting. Not this time. Backing out wasn't an option, even if I wanted to.

'You can't seriously want to spend Christmas alone,' she tried again. 'What about Mum and Dad? What about me?'

'Skipping the annual tour of emotional baggage?' I asked, counting socks. 'Stop at Dad's for eggnog that's eighty per cent whisky while he complains about Mum and Graham—'

'He's not that bad.'

'I know his drunken monologue word for word, and so do you. Then we leg it to Mum's, where she cries into her gin about not having grandkids, and Graham has a meltdown about the roast potatoes.'

'He didn't meltdown—'

'He threatened to *deep-fry* the turkey.'

She winced. 'Fine. But it's just what people do. You deal with your family quirks.'

'Not anymore, it was work or the Maldives. You could come with me?'

Megan sighed and set her mug on the table top. 'You can't keep hiding from them forever.'

'Watch me. I can, and I will. And I'll be bloody well paid to do so.'

The money was obscene. They'd wired the deposit

as if it were as insignificant as a fiver. Ten days of a *quaint* family stay at a manor house overlooking the sea. Private chef. Staff. Presents pre-wrapped according to my spreadsheet. I'd arranged a brass quartet because the brief said carols, but I doubted the local village had much more than a group of grannies with loft intentions about their talent. The hot chocolate wouldn't be powdered and dumped in a mug before being topped up by the kettle. I'd instructed the gardeners to source fresh mistletoe to artfully drape in photogenic doorways.

'I cannot believe you won't be home on Christmas Day,' Megan said, acting as if I'd said I was moving to Mars. 'Can't you do one day? Come for lunch at Dad's? We can time Mum's so we get her before the gin. You can nap in the car between houses. I'll drive. I'll bring snacks.'

'Tempting.' I folded another jumper. 'But no.'

'Amanda.'

I didn't look up.

'Megan. I'm not going to back down. Everything is arranged. I'm going to go and give my clients the kind of Christmas most people could only dream of. Then I'm going to invoice them until they cry festive tears. And then, in January, when everyone else is touting for work to see them through the month, I'll book a holiday somewhere with sun and no tinsel. That's *my* Christmas.'

'So you're replacing our family with strangers.'

'I'm replacing emotional warfare with controlled chaos. There's a difference.'

'They're millionaires,' she said, as if the word itself should rearrange my mind. 'Remember the wedding in Monaco? You came with that twitch.'

'That twitch paid for my deposit on this place, and the nice knives.'

Her eyes softened.

'Is this about...' she gestured vaguely.

My muscles seized. 'It's about work.'

'Mmm.'

Megan dug her toes under my rug and watched me stuff my life into zippable compartments.

'Tell me about them,' she said, accepting that I wasn't going to back down. 'This family. The clients.'

'Australian old money married new. He made something with an app.'

'Of course.'

'She runs a foundation. Then there's the grandmother who moved to Australia as a kid when her parents emigrated. She was brought up on a rural Scottish estate, and it's her urging that has them back here to celebrate Christmas. Three adult children with surnames for first names and careers that I don't fully understand. A heap of grandchildren. And there's a donkey.'

'A donkey.' Megan brightened. 'Well, at least someone will be there to smooch you.'

'I'm not kissing a client's donkey.'

'You're so lame.'

'I never said I wasn't.'

'Mum is going to ask where you are,' Megan said. 'Graham will offer to pick you up in the Volvo like we're ten. And you won't be here.'

'Correct.'

'And I'll have to say, Amanda had abandoned us for another family's Christmas, and she'll give a sad smile and say she's happy for you, and then she'll pour an extra-large gin. And you know what gin brings.'

'Tears.'

Megan pressed her fingers against the edge of the table. 'You can't hide forever.'

'Forever is a stretch,' I said. 'I'm hiding for ten days. And I've already told Mum and Dad.'

'Christmas isn't that bad...'

'It's loud and fake, and people expect things from you,' I said. 'It thrusts you under mistletoe with men who can't take no for an answer. It drags out all my failings as the family probes me about why I haven't found another boyfriend yet. It makes Mum look at me like she's waiting for me to announce a miraculous conception, while I've only brought a bloody cheese board.'

Megan scrunched her nose. 'We love you, though.'

'I know. I love you all too. Just can't handle another Christmas in a misery sandwich.'

She reached for the little stack of gift tags on my dresser.

'Are these for them?' The tags were beautiful: thick cream card, hand-pressed lettering, my logo, a tiny golden monogram on the back—pale gold ribbon. No glitter.

'For place settings and presents. Gifts are purchased, wrapped, and weighted so they look generous but fit in cases to travel home. There's a Santa sack with their initials embroidered on it. The thing cost more than my first car. I've got the menus finalised and the alcohol signed off on. The tree is arriving with its own team, decorated in the soft golds and glassware that's in this season. We even have a full sleigh and a team of reindeer stopping by with a Santa who's flown in from Norway for the day.'

'A sleigh.'

'A real one. For photos.'

Megan grinned. 'You're going to hate how beautiful it is there.'

'Unlikely.'

'You are.' She flopped onto my bed and punched my spare pillow before stuffing it under her cheek. 'You'll get out the car and pretend not to notice the shimmer of the sea or the quaint little houses. Just hide behind your clipboard like an emotionless robot. You'll scowl at it all and then secretly fancy living there in about four days.'

I allowed myself half a smile. 'If I get any notions, I'll call you.'

We did the checklist dance. Passport, I always bring it; rich people can pivot destinations like they're ordering pudding. Charger. Chargers for the chargers. Contract file. Site maps. The emergency bag with needles, paracetamol, plasters, stain remover, safety pins, and my little black book of sources. The people who can get just about anything at the drop of a hat. For the right price, of course.

'Do you get a day off?' Megan asked, reading my schedule upside-down. 'At all?'

'I get hours that are less insane than others.'

'When will you call me?'

'Every time I can.'

She came around the bed and hugged me, which I

endured like a belligerent cat. 'I know you're doing what you need to, but you don't have to do it alone.'

'I'm literally taking a team.'

She squeezed, eyes shiny. 'Text me when you get there?'

'If I have signal.'

'If you don't, I'll assume a kelpie ate you and tell Mum you died doing what you loved, bossing people around.'

'I don't enjoy bossing people around.' I just happened to be good at it. If anything, it was exhausting.

' I hope Bayview Manor is haunted by a friendly ghost who teaches you the true meaning of Christmas.' Megan said as we battled my suitcase onto the floor.

'If I'm going to get haunted, it better at least be a hot ghost.'

two

OTTERLEIGH BAY VILLAGE NEWS
Who is in charge up on the hill? The one tending roses, or the one trying to eat them?

HENRY

THE TWENTY-FIRST OF DECEMBER WAS FINALLY UPON ME.

Being handed the keys for Bayview Manor felt as monumental as the first time my parents trusted me with a house key.

Albeit, I had no intention of stealing my bosses' vodka and watering it down to hope they wouldn't notice and dry humping girls on their sofa. Shame really, I was clearly far more interesting at seventeen than at present.

'Front door, side door, cellar. The rest of the keys are in the office lockbox if you need to open the other entrances. You have the greenhouse and outhouse ones already.' Lord Leadbetter, or Fenton as he preferred us to call him, dropped the keys into my palm with a resounding clunk. If someone pounced on me in the dark, I didn't doubt they could double as a medieval-looking weapon.

'Don't worry, I'll look after the place for you,' I reassured the older man, hitting him with a sunny smile that I hoped would assuage his apprehension. Usually, their butler took the helm, but he'd had to go home to look after his ailing mother, so they were entrusting the place to me. I had little doubt about how the outside world perceived me. Silly, goofy, smiley, a bit of an airhead. I'd always found that life was a little less hard when attacking it with happiness. But it didn't mean I couldn't step up. I worked hard and always surpassed expectations. Hell, making people happy had become my favourite pastime.

'Oh, Fenton, stop havering. The car's waiting.' Lady Leadbetter swept through the hall in her ever grandiose style, planting a lipstick-marking kiss on my cheek. 'Look after Merv for me, won't you?'

'He'll keep me right, don't worry.' I laughed as Lady L.'s eyes glittered.

'Don't forget his Christmas basket. It'll arrive on

Christmas Eve.' She stood by the open door and shivered.

'You'll spoil that donkey.' Gooseflesh danced up my arms as a cold wind whipped through the door.

'I think it's too late for that,' Fenton said with a roll of his eyes.

He wasn't wrong. Their kids had grown up and left home, making their way in places far more exciting than Otterleigh Bay, so Lady L. adopted creatures to fill the void in her very empty home. Merv the donkey. Rascal the Great Dane. Numerous mousing cats. Rascal had been relocated for the week to stop him from sitting on the incoming client's knees and drooling on their supper, but Merv and I would be buddies. I could sneak out and have coffee with him whenever things in the house got too wild. I had little doubt that with high-paying customers and highly paid planners and designers, things would become frustrating real fast once the chaos descended. So I'd hide out in his stable like some nativity of avoidance.

Lady L. gripped a suitcase so small it could only be ornamental. A courier had already escorted their luggage ahead of them.

'Have a fantastic time, you'll have a blast catching up with your kids.' I followed them out and held out an arm to escort Lady L. down the stone front steps. She gave a wicked grin as she gripped my bicep.

'Stop fondling the staff, Dear,' Fenton groaned, the noise laced with humour. 'Save all that for me.'

Lord Leadbetter tutted at him. 'You've got the run of the place, son. Try not to burn it down while we're gone.'

'You have my word,' I said, which made Lady L. sigh into her scarf and mutter.

They bundled into the car, waving as though they were heading off for a world tour, not just two weeks in England. I stood on the front steps jingling my briefly inherited keys while the wind gripped me in ghostly, icy fingers. Bayview Manor stood silently behind me, all grand architecture and ancient stone.

'Well,' I told the house, 'just you and me for a bit. Until chaos descends.'

The manor creaked in what I chose to interpret as agreement.

I took a quick tour of the manor to ensure everything was in order. Fires stocked with wood and kindling, Christmas trees topped up with water and ready for the whirlwind of decor, and wreaths fluffed to accentuate their fullness. The orangery smelt gloriously citrus, the warmth cranked up to fight the growing chill outdoors. The boiler purred like a satisfied cat, well fed and content. Walking through the quiet halls enveloped me in the scent of wood polish and pine from the abundance of real garlands and trees.

Six trees.

The main Christmas tree stood in the entrance hall, twelve feet tall and fat as could fit in the double stairwell. It lurked sad and empty as it awaited adornment. I could picture it glittering, stuffed with baubles and trinkets, tinsel, and bows. Our Christmas tree at home was a mix of bought ornaments and years' worth of poorly made items brought home from school or clubs. Mum hung them up every year as though they were the most precious decorations in the box.

God, I fucking love Christmas.

The cheesy songs, the twinkling everything, the rich food and silly games. It pained me to miss it with my family, but since my siblings married and had children, it added a layer of complexity. Our core family faded as theirs took hold. I didn't blame them, it was the natural way of things, but Mum, Dad and I were carted from family to family as the years passed, until finally we'd given up and relocated Christmas until the twenty-ninth.

Satisfied with the state of the place, I poured a

coffee, grabbed a handful of carrots, and went to find Merv.

My donkey friend loitered in his stable, despite the gate being open to the yard. With two hoof prints in the frost, he must have stepped out before thinking hell no. Who could blame him? Musty hay aroma hung in the air as I sat on a stool inside the door. Merv's ears pricked as he gave a soft bray and walked over to meet me.

'Morning, Your Majesty,' I said, rubbing between his ears. 'How's the kingdom today? Bit frosty? Agreed.'

He snuffled hot air against my coat pocket, already homing in on the veggies hidden there.

'Alright, you greedy lump, move back and I'll give you the carrots.' Merv huffed until I produced the goods, then took them one at a time, chomping merrily, as we chatted. 'So that's the bosses gone for a little while, and soon the chaos descends. I'm not sure what they'll be like, but from the twenty thousand emails I must have gotten from the event planner, I'm estimating a pain in the ass.'

After Merv finished his carrots, I poured hot water into his feed bucket and stirred in Ribena. Merv shoved me out of his way, his muzzle sinking into the bucket with all the enthusiasm of a granny having her first sherry of Christmas Day.

'Cheers,' I said, lifting now cooling mug. 'To surviving whatever madness descends when the millionaires arrive.'

As I locked the stable back up when Merv retreated to the rear wall instead of following me out, a bright yellow bobble hat appeared at the fence.

'Morning, Henry!'

Lisa Baxter, or the bee lady as she's known locally, gripped the top of the fence with matching yellow mittens as her face came into view. She was all pink cheeks and nose, giving her usual ethereal charm some cosiness. I liked Lisa, and we often chatted over the fence while she tended her bees and I looked after the expansive manor gardens. There was no denying she was a bit odd, with her quiet and somewhat disarmingly wide stare, her gangly frame and her largely isolated lifestyle, but I found it only added to her vibe. She was also kind and thoughtful, and the first to offer help if ever I needed it. Help and honey.

'Morning yourself,' I called. 'How's your aunt today?'

'Same as yesterday, really. Got her all cosied up in bed with this cold snap setting in. It's a little easier now that she has nurses in to help once a day. Takes a bit of the strain. Got to check the hives and make sure the girls are tucked up too.'

Lisa runs her apiary with a gentle touch. The bees are adored, not merely a part of her shop's process, but the heart of the operation. Often, I could hear her voice lilting beyond the fence as she sang to them in a song that sounded older than the hills themselves. I'd never asked her the meaning of it in case it made her shy to know I could hear her singing. And I didn't want to deprive the bees of that sweetness.

She nodded toward the stable. 'Keeping Merv company, then?'

'He's keeping me company for my morning brew.' I held up my mug and smiled.

'So you're holding the fort for a while?'

'The Leadbetters have gone off to see their kids, so it's just me until the paying guests and the organisational dragon arrives. Already dreading working with her. Hoping she'll relegate me to the greenhouse.'

'Brave soul.'

'I'm being paid to babysit the manor and chat to a donkey. It could be worse.'

Her mouth twitched into a small smile. 'Not heading home for the holidays, then?'

'After Christmas,' I said. 'Family do for Betwixtmas. Easier once all my sisters have survived their in-law duties. How about you? Got anyone coming for the turkey?'

'No. Just Aunt Lucy and me again this year. The rest of the family are older and it's not so easy for them to travel up.'

She was an angel for the way she looked after her aunt. Returning her taking Lisa in as a child and bringing her up surrounded by bees, books and kindness. But it had to be hard. As far as I understood, her aunt was confined to bed and could barely communicate these days. Lisa spent hours reading to her and helping look after her, and never once complained.

'I won't be having dinner with the incoming family, but the staff will all grab something to eat together when the chaos settles on Christmas Day. If you can sneak away, you are more than welcome to join us.'

Lisa bit her lip as though it wasn't just popping next door but some huge invite. 'That's a lovely offer.'

'Not just an offer,' I said, smiling. 'It'll be great to chat without a fence between us, and we'll have more food and drink here than we could hope to get through. Plus, that's what friends are for.'

'Friends?' Lisa mouthed the word as though it were an alien concept. While we may not have hung out, ever, we spoke often in the years I'd worked at the manor.

'I hope we're friends.'

'Thank you. I'll see if I can sneak away for a little while in the evening. It would be nice to have a change of scenery.'

Merv brayed loudly, clearly agreeing.

'See?' I said. 'He demands you come over and meet everyone properly.'

Lisa nodded. 'Well, if Merv demanded it...'

'He does. See you on the 25th, Lisa.'

She raised a gloved hand. 'Not promising anything.'

Tucking my mug into the greenhouse, I donned my thickest gloves and wheeled a barrow of salt and grit round to the front steps.

I salted them thoroughly while humming Christmas tunes under my breath. The sun hung low in the sky, barely making it above the horizon for more than a few hours. Around two, the light would turn the estate gold for five perfect minutes before winter darkness swallowed it.

By the time I'd finished salting all of the entrances

and the connecting paths, I had grown sweaty, achy and frozen through.

The claw-footed bath in my en-suite called to me. With extra bubbles. And maybe a dram on the side.

It would be a blissful reprieve until business descended.

three

> OTTERLEIGH BAY VILLAGE NEWS
> Rumour has it there's a black cat in the village. But is her scratch all a show?

AMANDA

The taxi wasn't made for the insane back roads that led to the manor. Or I hoped they led there at least. If not, I might cry.

Horizontal rain lashed the windscreen, the wipers going ten to the dozen and still barely clearing it. When I'd stood at the train station waiting for the cab, the wind had felt cold enough that it could peel skin.

We pulled into a village that I'm sure would look charming if it weren't for the lashing rain and howling wind.

'Just going to see if I can get directions to make sure we take the right road,' the driver said. I shrank into the back seat when he opened the window, a gust of cold hitting me, and shouted to an older couple who were braving the weather, coats zipped up to their noses and looking like large, wet beetles.

'Can you direct us up to Bayview Manor?' he asked, holding his hand up to stop the rain from hitting his glasses.

He needn't have bothered. Within half a second, two cold faces appeared at the window, blocking the wind. While thankful for the lack of cold, their getting so close was a bit forward.

'Oh, who's this?' The old woman said, unzipping her coat enough to talk. She had a sweet, round face, reddened from the chill. I remained silent, awaiting her answer to the taxi driver's request.

The driver looked as disconcerted as I, leaning to the left in his seat to make a little space between them.

'Love, are you in to help with the fancy folk hiring Bayview for the holidays?'

'Um, yeah,' I said, looking to the driver to rescue me.

'Oh, lovely. Such a smashing place. Working on Christmas is unusual though, no family?'

'I'm not sure that's any of your business.' I hadn't meant to sound as sharp as I did, but who the hell was this nosy old bat?

She didn't flinch. 'Sorry, that was rude of me. I'm Morag, and this is Alistair. If you need anything, pop down to the village, and we'll get you sorted out.'

My face heated as she turned to the driver and gave him the directions before waving us off. Village life gave me the heebie jeebies. Everyone knowing everyone and all their business... gross.

The driver grunted around a mint humbug a few minutes later as we passed through an impressive set of gilded gates. 'Big place. Go family here?'

I gave a tight smile. 'Work.'

He grimaced. 'Rather you than me. I've taken Christmas off this year. It was that or suffer a month of the wife's wrath.'

We rounded a bend and saw Bayview Manor in all its glory, a sprawling, gleaming granite marvel. I opened a spreadsheet on my phone—one of many—and armed myself with the timings it contained. The clients didn't arrive until the evening, so I had the full day to ensure every little detail was perfect. The decorators should have been in for hours and were scheduled to finish at any moment.

I swallowed the bubble of guilt that rose in my

chest, spiky and horrid. Despite my assurances to my sister that I was totally fine to work over the holidays, doubt remained. No doubt on whether I cared about missing Christmas festivities, I'd grown to dread them with the familial infighting, but I wasn't so hard against my mum's hurt feelings. Nor my dad's disappointment.

I'd just have to keep myself busy.

I paid the driver, who deposited my suitcase on the gravel drive without an ounce of care. Straightening my shoulders, I started up the drive, dodging puddles and breathing in air so utterly fresh it was hard to believe it was real. Woodsmoke and sea salt clung to the chill, along with the lingering scent of evergreen.

The wheels of my suitcase stuttered in the gravel, lurching like an unruly dog.

'Not right now,' I threatened, pulling it while muttering a litany of curses below my breath. As I reached the steps, my hair sticking to my face and sweat gathering at my nape, a clunk sounded above me.

The door swung open.

A blond-haired man who rendered me momentarily frozen.

Tall and broad, visual perfection in human form.

Blonde curls, blue eyes, and a face as open and smiley as a golden retriever.

He practically hopped on the spot, and his cheerfulness doused my initial impression with a bucket of cold water. 'You must be Amanda.'

God help me.

'Indeed,' I said, gripping my suitcase handle a little tighter.

'I'm Henry, gardener, dogsbody, and current keeper of the keys.'

Of course he was.

'Lovely,' I said, stepping back as he bobbed down the steps with a wild grin. 'Where can I—'

He reached for my suitcase.

'I've got it,' I insisted.

'Really? It looks heavy.'

'I've. Got. It.'

He froze mid-reach, blinking at me with polite confusion, as if it were perfectly normal to be handing my luggage off to strangers. 'Right. Of course.'

Henry walked back up the stairs before turning to lean against the doorframe, watching me with devilry in those blue eyes. I hauled my far-overfilled suitcase up a step, flushing at the grunt I made. Determination drove me onwards as Henry watched, amusement dancing on his face.

I bit my lip to stop the next grunt from escaping.

I pushed past him into the hall, warmth surrounding me as I tried not to puff in my breath.

And then I saw it.

The tree.

Calling it a tree felt wrong. It wasn't a bloody tree, it was... monstrous. Twelve feet of headache-inducing sparkles and colour. Red and blue and glitter covered its branches like it had drunk Christmas and puked it back up. Tartan ribbons. Candy canes. Sparkling reindeer. Baubles of every shape and size.

It looked like a Quality Street tin had exploded.

'Oh God,' I breathed.

Henry followed my gaze, hands on his hips, practically glowing with pride. 'She's a beauty, isn't she?'

'She's... *something*,' I agreed, my brain twitching. The millionaires were expecting sleek, curated minimalism, not that abomination. 'The decorators are still here, right?'

His brow furrowed. 'Yeah, they are dealing with some of the garlands.'

'Oh, thank god. All of this,' I signalled to the tree, 'needs redoing.'

His face blanched. 'They've worked so hard on it.'

'That doesn't matter, it's not what I asked for. It's as far from sleek as humanly possible.'

I set off, vaguely knowing my way from the floor plans I'd meticulously studied. Henry followed behind me.

The decorators showed some resistance until I pulled up the emails with the detailed images and instructions I'd sent. At that point, they agreed that they must have sent the van with my decorations to a nearby wedding venue. With some strong insistence and additional hourly funds, they promised to get it rectified by supper time, just in the knick of time.

By the time I made it back to my abandoned suitcase, my blood rushed and my face heated.

Henry was smiling at me, framed by the gawdy tree, like we were in a Christmas advert. 'Tea?'

'No, thank you.'

'Coffee?'

'No.'

'Mince pie?'

'Absolutely not.'

He frowned. 'You don't like mince pies?'

'I don't like Christmas food,' I said crisply. 'Or Christmas music. Or tinsel. Or—'

He looked genuinely appalled. 'You don't like *Christmas*?'

I adjusted my scarf. 'Professionally, I love Christmas. Personally, I find it... tiresome.'

'Tiresome?'

'Yes. And sticky. And full of people who demand cheerfulness from everyone around them.'

'Ah, people like me.'

I blinked at him. 'What?'

'Coming at you with cheer, mildly sticky. Tiresome, some might say. You were describing me, weren't you?'

I opened my mouth, then shut it again.

He took a step closer, that smile never faltering. 'You've got the look.'

'What look?'

'Of a grinch.'

'I—excuse me?'

'You'll come round,' he said, maddeningly confident. 'Just like he did. Bit of mulled wine, a kiss under the mistletoe. Boom. Spirit of Christmas.'

I stared at him. 'I'm not kissing you.'

He laughed, the sound rich and warm and infuriating. 'I never said you would be, but nice to know you thought of me first.'

'So funny,' I said, fighting the urge to strangle him. 'Can you show me to my room, please?'

'Of course,' he said brightly, turning on his heel and walking straight into a hanging wreath.

The entire thing came down like an avalanche.

'Oh, for fuck sake.' I lunged to grab it, but the ribbon loop caught on my wrist.

He tried to catch the garland at the same time, meaning we both ended up in some kind of festive tug-of-war. I glared. He laughed.

I tried to stop the redness flushing into my cheeks. But I saw his eyes snag there as he unhooked the holly from my coat.

Then he leant in and grinned, making my blood pressure spike. 'This is going to be fun.'

'I doubt it,' I said, pulling the wreath from his hands and hanging it back on the wall.

Behind me, he whistled *Let It Snow* as my fingers tightened among the greenery.

four

```
OTTERLEIGH BAY VILLAGE NEWS
Golden retriever drools. Someone find a
      wet floor sign for the hall.
```

HENRY

By nine pm, the driveway looked like a Tesco car park on Christmas Eve.

SUVs lined up nose-to-tail, drivers opening doors, voices echoing across the courtyard. Children in matching red coats, and adults who looked preened to perfection and not like they'd spent twenty-four hours travelling. There was enough luggage piled neatly at the bottom of the stairs to clothe a village. I guessed being the bellboy likely fell to me.

And in the middle of it all stood Amanda Inglis. The sharply tailored, inappropriately heeled, neatly ponytailed figure of interest. Despite the perfectly coiffed millionaires departing the cars, she gleamed like a rare gem amongst them.

I couldn't even explain why. It wasn't like she'd been nice to me, not even personable, really. But her sharp little tongue ignited something deep inside me. Some feral urge that craved to know more about her.

'Henry, could you help with the luggage? They are all labelled with the room names.' She secured a label to the last case and looked at me expectantly.

Her tone was polite, but frosty.

I gave her a cheery grin, enjoying how much it seemed to irritate her. Merv brayed off in the distance, sensing upheaval. I liked to think he was backing me up.

One of the children, a little girl of around seven, looked me up and down as I descended the stone stairs. 'Are you the butler?'

The accent? Adorable.

'No,' I said. 'I'm the gardener.'

She frowned. 'In winter?'

'In winter, we prepare for next year.'

She scrunched her nose. 'Can I see the donkey?'

'After everyone is settled,' I promised. 'He'll be delighted to make a new friend.'

Amanda shot me a look, as though her fun detectors started flashing the minute someone dared to smile.

'Henry,' she said crisply, crossing the gravel like an angry cat. "Could you *please* get the cases in?"

Damn. I imagined making her moan *pleases* in far more interesting ways.

'Of course,' I said. 'Wouldn't want the bags getting cold.'

'Be serious.'

'Never.' I bit back a grin.

She rolled her eyes and turned away, already onto the next thing on her eye-watering list of tasks and times. Watching her was like watching someone conduct an orchestra. Every single movement of hers was meticulous.

I'd seen efficient people before, but I'd never seen anyone so bloody uptight with it.

She moved fast, but precisely. Petite, dark-haired, dark-eyed. Deliciously out of reach.

I'd be lying if I said it wasn't mesmerising.

I'd never met anyone less in need of help. Or less inclined to accept it. Yet, I wanted to find a way to see what her smile would be like. To see her loosen up and laugh. To hear her moan those pretty pleases in my ear as I...

Shit.

I lifted a case in front of my crotch and hobbled up the stairs. I didn't need anyone catching me with a boner in front of the clients.

'Down boy,' I whispered to myself as I lugged the case into the house and up the stairs. A task straining my muscles enough under the enormous weight of the bag, only further impeded by my current condition.

The eldest adult son, Raif, brushed past me when I eventually finished dragging the bags to each room as labelled, phone glued to his ear, and muttering something about the Wi-Fi. Amanda intercepted him like a heat-seeking missile. 'You'll find the password printed in the guest welcome pack I've left in each bedroom.'

He blinked. She gave a perfunctory smile before clipping away across the tiled floor.

I caught myself grinning.

'Why are you smiling?' Pru, the housekeeper, asked.

'Amanda frightens me,' I said. 'It's delightful.'

Pru snorted. 'You've got odd taste, she looks like she's sat on a bloody wasp.'

'She's like a cat who'd scratch you for thinking

about petting her, but you'd still want to win her over anyway.'

Pru chuckled and headed off toward the kitchen, muttering something about idiots and hormones.

Left alone, I did my best to be useful. Every so often, I'd glance up and spot Amanda, phone in one hand, clipboard in the other.

Thriving on order and control.

And yet, when one of the younger staff brought in to help out with serving accidentally dropped a tray of champagne flutes, she didn't shout at him. She just exhaled and said, 'Sweep it up. Quickly. Before anyone sees.'

Then she got to her knees and helped.

And that spiked my blood pressure. Seeing a potential soft side of her. Seeing her there, on the floor...

Warding off another raising of the flagpole, I fetched the sweeping brush and helped. By the time the glass was cleaned, the clients had retired to bed, leaving most of the staff to drift home for the night.

I leaned on the kitchen doorway, arms folded. 'You survived the first night.'

She jumped slightly, turning toward me. 'What are you doing?'

'Admiring you.'

'You're so odd,' she said.

'Just trying to see if your face ever cracks a genuine smile.'

Her eyes flicked over me briefly, dancing with something that could have been heat, and then dismissed me entirely. 'If you're not busy, you could resalt the paths. The weather app says we are due for a freezing night.'

'Yes, ma'am.'

She paused. 'Don't call me ma'am.'

'Right you are… boss.'

'Not that either.'

'Captain?'

She gave me a look that could've wilted my entire greenhouse. 'Goodbye, Henry.'

And off she went again, dark ponytail swishing, my poor heart trying to follow along behind her.

That odd tug in my chest came back—the fascination with the angry little cat.

She was pricklier than a cactus trapped in a holly bush. Every inch of her screamed *Do not touch*.

And yet…

There was something behind those narrowed eyes and spikey demeanour that said, *Convince me to climb into your lap and I'll purr for you.*

She'd fight it, of course. Probably come like the sweetest thing and then stab me with a pen for making her let go of her control.

I itched to find out.

The thought lingered, warm and stupid, as I stepped outside into the cold.

five

> OTTERLEIGH BAY VILLAGE NEWS
> Forecast: Hard wood and sore ankles

AMANDA

THE DAY'S PLAN WAS SIMPLE.

Get up before the clients.

Check the day's schedule.

Email the catering team with the clients' last-minute changes.

Absolutely, under no circumstances must I think about the *relentlessly* cheerful gardener.

The gardener whose forearms had inspired utterly indecent thoughts while I tossed and turned in bed the previous night.

I intended to avoid him at all costs. I didn't need a human-shaped dog trailing around judging me.

Unfortunately, the universe had a sick sense of humour.

I couldn't find the floral arrangements for the breakfast table, and the florist told me she'd left them in the greenhouse in water to keep them looking their best. So I pulled on a pair of Wellington boots at least four sizes too large, and headed out into the cold morning air to locate them.

A rhythmic thunk thunk thunk as I approached the greenhouse piqued my interest.

I should've kept walking. But curiosity got the better of me.

I followed the sound around to the left of the greenhouse and stopped dead at the sight that awaited me.

Henry.

Shirt sleeves rolled to his elbows, a mossy green jumper slung over a pile of frost-covered logs, and a long axe gripped in his calloused finger. Those blonde curls were damp around his forehead with effort, his breath fogging in the cold air as he brought his arms up and slammed the awaiting log, splitting it in two.

Damn. I'd like him to split me in two.

Fuck. No. That thought could take a long walk off a short plank.

Still, the way his forearms corded with veins had me clenching my thighs. Henry might act like a goofy pet, but he looked like he'd walked straight off the cover of an old bodice ripper.

He paused to wipe his brow with his forearm, and I found myself biting my lower lip. Then, he placed the next log, his thumb skimming the face of the wood. Those veins shifted under his skin, and I accidentally let the tiniest of moans escape.

Oh no.

Heat shot straight through me, sharp and wild.

It was absurd. I didn't even *like* him.

Not my type. I liked men with a sharper edge...

Still, my brain betrayed me with dirty little thoughts.

What would it feel like to let Henry handle me like he handled the wood?

Nope. Absolutely not. Delete that thought.

I turned to leave before I got caught moaning again, but my oversized boot caught on a plant pot, sending me arse over tit onto the frozen paving slabs.

One undignified yelp later, I sat on the ground, clutching my ankle through the rubbery traitors.

'Everything all right there?'

Of course he'd heard me.

Henry crouched beside me, all big blue eyes and thick fingers.

'Don't move,' he said, his calm demeanour almost commanding. I folded like a cheap deck chair.

'I'm fine,' I lied. 'Just tripped.'

'Right,' he said, smiling a little. 'So you're holding your ankle for emotional support?'

He reached out a hand. 'Come on.'

'I can get up myself.'

'You could,' he said, 'but you'll just hurt it more. Stop being so pig-headed and let me help you.'

Before I could protest, he scooped an arm under mine and half-lifted, half-guided me toward the greenhouse. It had been bad enough watching him from afar, but being pressed up against his warm side had my stomach flipping.

'Honestly,' I said, 'this is unnecessary.'

'Humour me.'

He eased me down onto a wooden bench among rows of plants and glass jars filled with cuttings.

'Right,' he said, crouching again. 'Let's have a look.'

'That's not—'

He was already gently tugging off the boot.

'Sit still,' he murmured, and a ribbon of heat filled me. My sock followed, and when his thumb skated my ankle, it took everything in me to avoid my face giving me away.

His hand wrapped gently around my ankle, steady and warm, as he turned it this way and that. He wasn't remotely inappropriate, unfortunately. It was attentive.

But my insides didn't care about that. Every nerve ending in my body lit up like a gaudy shopping centre Christmas tree.

'Does that hurt?' he asked, looking up.

His eyes were the exact colour of the winter sky on a clear day, and one curl hung down to graze his brow. I wanted to tuck it away, but daren't move.

I swallowed. 'No.'

He raised a brow.

'Well, maybe a little.'

Why did I feel so undone around him? When he looked up at me, it sent my groin into a tizzy. Inexplicable.

'It's just a twist,' he said, his fingers remaining against my skin. 'You'll be all right. Bit of rest, bit of ice.'

His fingers pressed once, testing the joint, and my pulse quickened. When I inhaled sharply, he narrowed his eyes at me.

'Pain?' he asked.

I swallowed hard and shook my head. Those blue eyes darkened just enough to slap me out of whatever nonsense I indulged in.

Standing, I winced at the cold ground beneath my naked foot and cleared my throat. 'Thanks, but I really must get on. Will you grab the floral centrepieces from the greenhouse and bring them indoors, please?'

'Of course.' Henry stood as I took my boot and pulled it back on before walking past him, ignoring the ache in my ankle.

'And Amanda?' I turned as he said my name, the sound adding another ribbon of heat. 'Next time you want to watch me chop wood, maybe do it from a safe distance, yeah?'

Mortification exploded in my chest. 'I was not watching you.'

He stepped closer to me, reaching out and running his thumb over my jaw. I should have stepped back, told him to fuck off, but I couldn't help myself. I tipped my head just a fraction into his touch.

'I enjoyed being watched by you.'

That gravelly voice. That infuriating calm. He

looked down at me, head tilted, eyes filled with soft amusement. 'You okay?'

'Fine,' I lied.

Then he left me there, all topsy turvy and both infuriated at his gall, and wet as his brazenness.

Maybe the puppy had teeth after all.

six

> OTTERLEIGH BAY VILLAGE NEWS
> NEWS: Unclaimed champagne left at the Tipsy Otter. If unclaimed, expect sore heads.

HENRY

By afternoon, Amanda was in a tizzy all over again. The champagne had been mistakenly delivered to the local pub, and she insisted we retrieve it at once.

Not that I minded an afternoon pub trip.

The *Tipsy Otter* was already heaving by the time I pulled up in the ancient Land Rover, which was more duct tape than anything else. The village glowed, all golden windows, misted glass, and the bubble of merriment from within the busy pub.

Amanda stiffened in the passenger seat, tugging her coat tighter around her. 'It looks busy.'

'It's nearly Christmas, the place will be stuffed until January third after Hogmany.'

Amanda frowned. 'Sounds ghastly. We're just collecting the champagne, no socialising.'

'Course, quick in, quick out. No danger of actually enjoying anything remotely festive.'

She shot me a look. 'I do enjoy things. Just not festivities. There's nothing wrong with that.'

'I mean, you've made the Christmas trees at the manor look like a sad, beige forest.' I probably shouldn't poke the bear, but I couldn't help myself.

'Just because you know nothing about style, doesn't mean the rest of the world wants that. I'm paid for my opinions, *you are not.*' The village lights reflected on her grumpy face, and I bit back a smile.

'I give my opinions for free, aren't you lucky?'

The village looked like a Christmas postcard. Fairy lights looped from lamppost to lamppost, and the cute coloured doors were decked with wreaths. A glistening frost gazed over everything in a glittering layer.

Stepping out of the Land Rover had nearly ended with me on my arse, grabbing the door at the last second to steady myself.

'Wait a minute,' I shouted through the car to Amanda, who hesitated halfway out of the seat.

I made my way around the car, testing the slippery cobbles until I became confident enough in my step.

Amanda bristled as I held out a hand.

'I nearly fell, trust me, it's better to accept a little help than end up with a bruised arse.'

She sighed and slid her hand into mine.

My world lurched at that small contact, the warmth creating a fire that whipped through me. I froze for a few seconds too long, and awkwardness descended over us. She cleared her throat and raised her eyebrows, kickstarting my pulse.

'Come on then,' I said, as though it were she delaying her exit, and not me, half falling in love with a singular handhold.

As soon as she stepped inside, she dropped my arm, much to my dismay. The entire pub turned to look, and I waved.

An uncharacteristic quietness thrummed in the pub as eyes moved from me to the pretty, dark-haired woman beside me. Interest sparkled through the room nearly as brightly as the glistening of the tinsel. Tinsel, which I was convinced they'd reused since the 80s.

Amanda froze beside me before setting her shoulders straight and walking confidently toward the bar. An unstoppable force.

The Harris family sat squeezed around a table, Owen waving before setting his arm back around Claire. Isla looked half-way to sozzled, likely her first big night out since having her baby, and Jeff sat nursing his beer and taking slightly terrified glances at her. Eilidh, Emma and Lola sat at the bar, like a gaggle of giggling geese, while Morag and Alistair sat with the other senior members of the village, Morag waving wildly at Amanda.

Kenny, the owner, looked up with a smile on his well-reddened face. 'Managed to pull yourself out of the greenhouse for a pint? Who's your pal?'

Before I could open my mouth, Amanda cleared her throat. 'I'm Amanda Inglis, and I don't need him to speak for me. I'm managing an event at Bayview Manor. There's been a delivery mix-up—'

'Aye, that'll be the champagne, we thought it was a Christmas miracle until the suppliers called. Sounds like you tore them a new one,' Kenny said, nodding toward the back. 'Landed here by mistake this morning. I'll get the lads to stick it in your truck. But you'll sit for a minute first. Can't have you standing there looking like you've got a chill.'

'That's really not necessary.' Amanda glanced toward the door.

'Sit doon and stop your fussing,' he said, and that was that.

Amanda hesitated, clearly debating whether to argue. I leaned in, dropping my voice. 'One drink won't kill you.'

And before she could talk herself out of it, I placed a hand on the small of her back, guiding her forward. She stilled under my touch for a heartbeat before softening enough to move.

She shook me off as she took the seat at the bar, giving me a wickedly sour look. Lord, I wanted to wipe that anger off her face. Kiss her until she learned how to smile.

Kenny poured two mulled ciders from the pot. 'On the house. It'll warm you right up while we sort your champagne out.'

'Thank you,' she said stiffly, perched on the stool and looking around as the hubbub returned to normal levels of merriment.

The log burner roared in the corner, the smell of cinnamon and ale in the air. Dogs snored happily amongst boots as people went back to their quiz papers.

Morag shouted over, even she looking a little deep in her cups. 'Alright, lass, how are you settling in? Is it all champagne and fanciness up on the hill for you, or are you happy down with us regular folk?'

'Morag,' I said warningly, but Amanda surprised me.

'I prefer gin,' she said, perfectly deadpan.

Morag cackled. 'Oh, I like her.'

Amanda turned pink but held her head high, sipping the hot, spiced drink with restraint. The firelight caught in her dark hair, making it glow reddish at the edges. She seemed smaller in the pub than at the manor, where the moment she'd stepped into the building, she'd filled the space. It struck me with an urge to protect her, which was ridiculous, knowing her capabilities. Still, I clenched a fist to fight off the need to drape my arm around her waist.

'You alright?' I asked quietly.

'I'm fine,' she said.

'Indeed.' That had her giving me another look that screamed, "Behave yourself." But where's the fun in that?

Kenny reappeared, wiping his hands. 'Boxes are all sorted, hen. Cal and Danny'll load them into the truck for you.'

'Thank you, that's very kind of you.'

'Ach, kindness costs nothing,' Kenny said. 'Now

finish your drink before you've got to go back out in the cold.'

Amanda looked around, her shoulders relaxing despite herself.

'It's cosy in here,' she said.

'That's one word for it.'

She shook her head. 'You really love it here, don't you?'

'What can I say, the place gets under your skin.'

Her gaze lingered on the window, where the frost blurred the edges of the fairy lights outside.

'I'll take your word for it,' she murmured.

We sat in companionable quiet, me trying to find something to say while remaining tongue-tied. I'd always been plenty confident enough around women, so why did Amanda have me knotted like an old pair of laces?

I finally had her sat in one place instead of rushing from task to task, and found myself with nothing but thoughts that made my cheeks heat.

A minute later, Kenny gave us a wave. 'You're all set, love. Safe drive back.'

She stood, smoothing her coat. 'Thank you. You've been very welcoming.'

'Of course we have, we're nothing if not friendly in Otterleigh Bay,' Kenny said. That earned him a rare smile, which made jealousy flare in the pit of my stomach. I wanted all of her smiles.

I checked that the load was steady before closing the back door of the 4x4. Amanda stood by, coat wrapped tight and breath fogging in the cold air.

'All okay, boss?' I teased.

She glanced at me, features sharp. 'Just thinking it's not so bad here, maybe.'

On the drive back up the hill, she was quiet again as the village lights faded behind us.

I only had nine days left with her in command of the manor. I'd be damned if I wouldn't find a way to see her have some fun.

seven

> OTTERLEIGH BAY VILLAGE NEWS
> Is that smoke from the Manor chimneys, or someone's ears?

AMANDA

Somewhere between the third spilt drink and the fifth time I'd had to request the kids stop trying to slide down the bannisters, knocking garlands off as they did, my professional veneer started wavering. Despite the morning of clay shooting for the adults, and the puppeteer for the children, it's like the clients were going stir crazy in the manor.

By lunchtime, I'd mediated two arguments between the chef and Pru, the housekeeper, and narrowly prevented a seven-year-old from dismantling a taxidermy badger to see whether it still contained its *insides*. I'd relocated the badger to my office for safekeeping, and having his glassy-eyed stare dogging me meant hiding in there was no fun either.

Was the twitching in my left eyelid my imagination?

Honestly, I should be gifted an award for the fact that I hadn't snapped at anyone. Or torn some ancient, fancy curtains to shreds. Or threw a wellie boot through a window.

Yet. There was still time.

By three o'clock, the family had rejected my idea of a long walk together guided by Henry. Had sent away the watercolour artist who had been instructing them, and they seemed to be wandering the halls, giving me more things to stress about. Never had I had clients so utterly dissatisfied with the schedule we'd agreed on.

'Amanda, is there any vegan shortbread?' Despite no one being vegan, but Flora and Raif, the eldest set of the matriarch's heirs, had been feeling *bubbly.*

'Amanda, have you seen my daughter?' Which one? The one trying to bowl with a melon or the one terrorising Pru with twenty questions a minute?

'Amanda, why is the Wi-Fi so slow?' You're in rural Scotland... Everything's a bit slower-paced, especially the internet.

By four, I wondered if my smile looked as forced as it felt. I escaped to the bathroom and debated my professional grin until I no longer knew what my smile should look like. Probably not the way it did.

It was only when I realised the children had gone suspiciously quiet that I felt worry clawing at my stomach.

Quiet kids were often a part of the package with wealthy clients, many had long learned to be seen and not heard, or were shushed away by well-paid nannies, but not The Petersens. They'd left their nannies in Australia, and their children were taking full advantage of the feral opportunities.

The halls held no clues as to where the children had disappeared to.

'Mrs Petersen,' I asked, seeing the matriarch sitting by the fire while reading a book. 'Where are the children?'

'I'm not sure. They followed the gardener.'

'For a walk?'

'To see the donkey, perhaps. The children have been most excited to meet it.'

The donkey. Of course.

The air was bitingly sharp, a thin mist rolling up over the cliffs and emerging through the trees. I made my way around to the gardens as excited babbling met my ears. And there, like a cheery woodland sprite come chiselled Michelangelo statue, sat Henry.

Excitedly regaling some story, clippers in one hand, and a bundle of holly and pine in the other, those blond curls looked wilder than ever. A crate of colourful ribbons sat at his feet, spilling over like silken spaghetti. The six children clustered around him, eyes wide with sheer idolisation.

Merv the donkey stood amongst the chaos, chomping on a child's pine cuttings while she squealed in delight.

'Oh, good, even the donkey is here.'

Henry gave me one of those pulse-fluttering, sparkly-toothed smiles as I spoke. 'Afternoon, boss.'

'I am *not* your boss,' I muttered, stepping over green clippings and 'What exactly is happening here?'

'We're wreath-making, the kids were antsy, so I thought I'd put them to work.'

'They're guests, not elves.'

'We made paper chains too. And found a load of pom-poms and tinsel.' A child piped up, hair full of pine needles.

One of the twins held up a garish-looking sparkly bit of tat. 'Amanda! We're going to hang them on the big tree!'

I stared. And inhaled slowly. *Deeply*. Trying to find

some semblance of cool before I emitted enough flames to incinerate Henry.

'I don't think that's a good idea,' I said.

Before I could build my argument, Rita appeared, wrapped in a tartan shawl. Her eyes softened, wet around the edges and full of wonder.

'Oh, how lovely. It's just like when I was little.' she whispered. Her fingers danced over the multicoloured tinsel, tousled a child's hair and then petted Merv's snout.

Henry stood. 'Thought it might be a nice change of pace.'

'It's perfect.'

Which was when Merv turned his big old eyes on me.

Or rather... toward my coat.

My *very expensive, Italian, tailored coat that had cost me an absolute bomb, and I was still paying off monthly.*

'Don't even think about it,' I warned as he stepped closer, his lips reaching for my sleeve. I stumbled back and hit a wheelbarrow, barely catching myself. Giving the donkey time to nab the bottom of my coat.

'Absolutely not,' I said through gritted teeth, pressing a hand between his eyes and pushing firmly. He didn't budge.

Rita laughed as she patted his neck. 'Oh, he likes you.'

'He's likes to vex me,' I hissed.

Merv began chewing as I fought off the urge to cry. 'Henry, get your beast off of me.'

'Merv,' Henry said, half laughing. 'Mate, leave her coat alone.'

Merv ignored him.

'Henry?' I said through gritted teeth, stuck in place while a donkey attempted to ingest my designer tailoring.

'I am,' he said, coming over. 'I'm negotiating.'

'Negotiate faster.'

The children shrieked with laughter, their high-pitched noises only seeming to egg the donkey on.

'Developed a taste for quality, haven't you, pal?'

'Henry, please?' I pleaded, and Henry stood looking down at me, one hand on Merv's mane, and his eyes darkening at the plea in my voice. Leaning closer, he lowered his voice until it took on a gravelly depth that hit me right between the thighs.

'Well, since you begged so prettily, Amanda.'

Fuck. Where did that come from? And why did it remind me of the relationships I'd chased in my early twenties? I'd given up when all it brought me were guys who said they could play the games I craved, but actually just wanted a rougher BJ without any of the giving side of things. Just want want want. But surely Henry, the smiley golden retriever, wasn't into all that. Wishful thinking, perhaps.

With my head in the clouds and my pulse going ten to the dozen, I almost forgot the bloody donkey eating my coat. Henry finally managed to pry it free.

I looked down at the damaged edge, the material frayed and crumpled. Then up at him.

He winced. 'Could be worse.'

I closed my eyes for a second to recalibrate myself and plastered a professional look back on my face.

I ushered them all inside before someone lost a finger to the sharp clippers. The moment we reached the entrance hall, the children exploded upon it with armfuls of paper chains, oodles of ageing tinsel and decorations that had seen better days. Sticky fingerprints were as much a part of the result as the rest of the chaos. Someone dropped a pom-pom, and it rolled beneath the grand piano.

When they finished, I stared at the tree. My elegant, carefully curated, soft-gold Christmas tree.

A neon-green paper chain sat dead centre, like an alien worm.

'Oh,' someone breathed behind me.

I turned to find Rita standing near the stairwell, her hand over her heart and her face beaming.

'Would you look at that,' she said, hand drifting to her throat. 'It's been so long since I've seen a tree like this.'

I blinked. 'Like... this?'

'Chaotic,' she said warmly. 'Real. None of that sterile magazine nonsense. This is the Christmas I remember. The Christmas I want my grandchildren to have.'

I tried very, very hard not to look directly at Henry, who was leaning against a bannister looking like the cat who got the fucking cream. Hot or not, I wanted to kick him in the shins.

The children continued adding atrocities. Glitter appeared. Feathers. A bauble that had definitely not existed before today, containing what looked like three sequins and a tooth.

My seasonal palette was designed to evoke winter luxury. *Gone.* Drowned beneath pom-poms. The adults glanced at me, waiting for approval.

So I lied. With another fake smile.

'If you're happy, I'm happy.'

'It's perfect,' Rita said.

If she said perfect one more time while referencing the monstrosity before me, I might actually combust.

Henry moved closer, warmth rolling off him like he hadn't just been outdoors creating havoc.

'Not so bad, is it?' he murmured.

'It is. Very bad.'

'They're happy.' I followed his gaze to the clients, who did look happier than I'd seen them since they arrived.

'They're deranged.'

He leaned in, voice low enough to make me quiver. 'It's Christmas, Amanda. Maybe imperfection's allowed.'

'No, it's really not.'

But when the children burst into giggles as Rita proudly lifted their lopsided wreaths, something in me softened. A *tiny* bit. Enough that Henry caught it.

I scowled at him for good measure before sidling away from him.

'Hot chocolate?' I suggested, desperate for a distraction.

The children cheered.

Henry's lips quirked.

And I guided them into the parlour, my head feeling utterly stuffed with cotton wool as I bounced between annoyance and relief. Of course, I was pleased that the clients were happy, but did it mean I was bad at my job? I'd always excelled in making events magical.

Yet, Henry had come in and managed it with little more than a fucking frin and a box of old stuff from the attic.

eight

OTTERLEIGH BAY VILLAGE NEWS

It's all cream and lady fingers

HENRY

Freshly showered after putting Merv to stable for the night, I eyed my bed longingly. Entertaining six rambunctious children had taken it out of me. Still, it had been a good day. For the clients and me at least. Amanda had been throwing me daggers every time she had to walk past the newly decorated tree. I'd been trying to help keep her patrons happy, and somehow it had only made Amanda more prickly.

As I headed for the bed, a thought snuck in to ruin my pace. Had I locked the side door when I'd come in? While I was sure no ill would come to the house in the middle of the night, I didn't want to let the Leadbetters down. With a sigh, I dried off and pulled on my ridiculous Christmas jumper with the giant sparkly H on the front, given to me the previous Christmas by Jean Harris when I'd joined her family for Christmas Dinner. It was loud and garish, and it saddened me that I could only wear it a few times a year during the holidays. The entire Harris clan, the local whisky distillery owners, had all been wearing matching ones, and I'd never forgotten how welcoming I'd found it. Teamed with grey sweats and unlaced boots, I crept back downstairs to check the door, hoping not to disturb anyone.

All for nothing. The door was locked tight. Shaking my head, I made for my room, but paused as I neared the kitchen.

Something sweet and sugary filled my nostrils and had my mouth watering. But the kitchen should be closed. The chef had long headed home, ready for an early start.

I followed the aroma, like some sugar-scenting hound, straight into the kitchen.

Sweeping my gaze over the room proved fruitless. It lay empty and dark, but for the light about the range cooker. Had I imagined it.

Then a tiny metallic scrape sounded from beyond the kitchen counter. Treading lightly, I investigated.

Amanda Inglis sat on the kitchen floor in front of the ancient forest green Aga. Cross-legged and back slouched against a cupboard. Her hair balanced on top of her head in a squint and somewhat messy ponytail, while a red knitted cardigan sloped off one shoulder, revealing a dark vest top below. A vast, catering tray of sticky toffee pudding balanced on her knees, while a can of squirty cream sat beside her. I watched, transfixed as she sprayed a white blob onto the toffee sauce-covered sponge before shovelling a massive bit into her mouth.

She looked... unguarded. Soft around the edges in a way I'd not seen her. Like she'd left her barriers upstairs with her work clothes. My stomach clenched at the sight of her, and an urge to wrap her up and make her happy washed over me.

She took another bite. A slow one. Her eyes fluttered shut for half a second, like she was finally letting herself breathe. The warm orange light from the Aga lit up her pretty face, and a jolt of something hit me. Like I was intruding on something I wasn't supposed to see.

My chest squeezed so hard it stole my breath.

Then she spotted me.

The look on her face was pure caught-out schoolgirl, her shoulders tensing.

'Oh, for fuck's sake,' she groaned and dropped her head back against the cupboard.

'Don't stop on my account.'

'I couldn't sleep. I didn't think anyone was still up.'

'No one else, just me,' I said, moving to where she sat, clutching the enormous tray. 'But the smell of pudding called as I was checking the doors.'

Her chin lifted, those prickles resurfacing. 'Don't judge me. I'm too frazzled to deal with your mockery tonight.'

'I wouldn't dream of it.' I grabbed a spoon from the cutlery drawer and sat beside her. Her eyes widened as I leaned in and took a sizeable scoop before she could swat my hand away.

'You're not seriously—'

'Mmm.' I closed my eyes dramatically as I chewed. 'Bloody delicious.'

'You're an ass.'

'Possibly,' I said, stealing another spoonful. 'But at least I'm well-fed.'

That earned me a fraction of a genuine smile, even if a roll of her dark eyes accompanied it, and I wanted to snatch it up and keep it.

We sat in amicable silence for a while. Just sneaking spoonfuls of the cakey dessert like two kids hiding in a kitchen at a house party, stealing treats before anyone found us. I couldn't tell if the warmth filling me was from the Aga or my proximity to Amanda.

She looked different like this. Not the hyper-efficient version she showed the clients. The brittleness was softened, and with each bite, she unwound a little more.

Eventually, our eating pace slowed, and I felt the need to fill the empty space with words.

'Why do you hate Christmas so much?'

Her spoon paused mid-air. 'Who says I hate it?'

'Your face, primarily.'

She huffed, staring at the pudding. 'I don't hate it. I just never enjoy it. It's always been messy. Family fighting. People pretending things are fine when they're not. Mum crying. Dad drinking too much. Being carted from one house to another while trying to balance my parents' emotions. The whole festive performance. So this year, I bowed out of pretending.'

'By working a Christmas event?'

'Everyone talks about Christmas cheer,' she said quietly. 'I just get Christmas dread. This way, I can focus that into productivity, and go on a sun-soaked holiday in January when it's all finally over.'

'That's rough.'

She shot me a look. 'You're not going to tell me to cheer up?'

'Nope.'

'Or that family's what you make it?'

'Definitely not.' Her thigh relaxed against mine, and I froze, not wanting to move an inch in case it startled her away. 'Some families suck.'

'Well, I can agree on that. So why are you here instead of with your family if Christmas is so great?'

'We moved Christmas to the 28th.'

'You can't just move Christmas.'

'Who says? My sisters are all partnered and familied up, so it just makes it easier for everyone, and Mum and Dad get a day where they don't have to split their time of share. All the kids come home for a few days.'

'When you put it like that, I guess it makes sense. My sister and I are both single, so it's just us, and we're going from one house to another, trying to make everything even so no one feels left out.'

'Sounds exhausting. No wonder you hit veto this year.'

'Yeah. I love my job, and my family, despite everything, but I just get so tired.' Amanda placed the tray on the counter before flopping right back down beside me on the tiles.

'Tired of being in charge,' she murmured. 'If I stop to breathe, everything falls apart this time of year.'

I watched her fingers tease the button on her cardigan, turning it as she spoke. The small line between her brows as she vented.

'Do you always have to control everything? Or do you ever stop and just let yourself enjoy something?'

'I'm not a robot, but no, it's hard to let go when there's no one there to help take the slack. Then everything piles up and just makes it worse.'

I smiled. 'Maybe you should try letting someone take care of you for once?'

'Who?'

'Oh, I don't know. Maybe a fantastic, and handsome, gardener who knows how to take control long enough for you to enjoy yourself.' My brazenness was risky, but I couldn't help myself. Amanda would leave in a few days, and I wanted to lay my cards on the table before she did.

She blinked at me. And for a heartbeat, her guard slipped. Heat flickered in those dark eyes. Temptation. Desire. Excitement.

A bit of sauce glistened on her lip.

I reached out, my thumb skimming her mouth. Gathering up the sweetness, I tasted it.

Her breath caught, and the room tilted a little. Or maybe I did.

'Henry,' she whispered, half-warning, half-breathy need.

I leaned close enough to catch the warmth of her skin and the faint hint of perfume clinging to her cardigan. Her pupils darkened, which had my pulse escalating. For one perfect moment, strung with so much possibility, I breathed her in.

There was nothing more I wanted than to kiss her. To feel her lips lock with mine as I lost myself in her. To show her that it was okay to loosen the reins.

Then sanity clawed its way back in. She didn't even like me. Was I pushing myself on her in a moment of vulnerability? That wasn't me.

I exhaled sharply and pushed up to my feet. Kissing her might push her to somewhere that made her uncomfortable, and I didn't want to do something we'd both regret in the morning.

She stayed on the floor, looking up at me with her cheeks flushing.

'Night, Amanda,' I said, trying to sound relaxed, but my voice was decidedly hoarse.

I made for the corridor before I could change my

mind, pulling the kitchen door closed behind me. I made it to the centre hall, at the foot of the stairwell, before I stopped and cussed myself out for being a wimp.

I'd wanted to kiss her more than I'd wanted to breathe, but kissing Amanda would be about as sensible as letting Merv weed the vegetable patch.

Since when did we worry about sensible, Henry?

nine

OTTERLEIGH BAY VILLAGE NEWS
Mistle-I-told-you-so

AMANDA

I LOOKED LIKE A STICKY-FINGERED RACCOON, CROUCHED over the sink at nearly midnight while scraping toffee residue off the catering dish. I couldn't decide if it was the pudding sitting heavy in my stomach or the uneasiness of my time with Henry.

For a moment, I'd thought he was going to kiss me.

And for a moment, I would have let him.

Which left me feeling all kinds of topsy-turvy. I'd let him get close, and for what? For him to wipe my lip and leave?

What the fuck?

The thud of disappointment as he'd pulled away had caught me off-guard. When Henry pushed himself to his feet and walked out, leaving me on the floor with my pudding, I wanted to demand he come right back over and put his god damned tongue in my mouth.

I scrubbed harder, as though cleaning dishes could fix the disturbing void he'd left.

'Why do you even care?' I asked myself. 'He's not even your type. He's too cheery. Too hoppy. Too sweet. I liked men a little darker… in the bedroom at least.

Although Henry had said he knew how to take control and sent my thighs clenching, he probably didn't mean it how I hoped he did.

I should not be thinking about him.
Not like this.

Not with a warm, traitorous pull in my stomach.

But no matter how hard I scrubbed, the moment kept replaying in my head. Searching for what I'd done to make him leave. Was it my fault? Did my resting bitch face send him scarpering? Or had I imagined the heat in his eyes? No. It had been there. The way his thumb brushed my lips, like he was thinking about how they'd feel pressed against his. The way the air had thickened between us, growing heavy. The way he'd looked at me like he needed to taste...

I groaned as I dried up the dishes.

I should *not* be lusting after the gardener.

I should be focusing on work and my clients, not remembering Henry leaning toward me, smelling like freshly chopped wood and pine trees.

And yet.

A holiday fling wouldn't be the worst thing in the world, would it?

Not forever. Not feelings. Not complicated.

Just a few days of letting my nether regions overrule my brain. Letting the man-shaped golden retriever take control for ten minutes, hell, maybe longer if I'm lucky, wouldn't be so bad.

It would have to be top secret, of course. If he even wanted to.

I turned off the kitchen light with a sigh.

'Get a grip,' I muttered, resigning myself to the whole damned thing being in my head.

The hallway was steeped in darkness, the only light coming from the still-lit monstrous tree in the foyer. I rounded the corner and at the foot of the double stairwell, Henry stood, sleeves rolled up and leaning against the wall by the piano.

One of his feet was braced back against the

panelling, those thickly muscled arms folded. He tipped his head as I froze.

The puppy-dog vibes had vanished, replaced by something darker and more thrilling in his face. Something almost devilish that had heat coiling deep inside me.

'Everything alright?' I asked, swallowing down a whole bundle of nerves.

Henry didn't answer. He pushed off the wall and crossed the space, looking more like a tiger than a retriever. My breath hitched as the floor between us narrowed. I stepped backwards, my spine hitting the wall.

'You're doing rounds, checking lights. Doors. That sort of thing?' he asked.

'Just, uh, going to my, uh, bed.'

Come on, Amanda, you know how to bloody well speak.

Those icy blue eyes lifted to the space just above my head.

'You know, for someone who hates Christmas, you've picked an interesting place to stop.'

'Why?' I followed his gaze.

Mistletoe.

Jeez Louise. Who the hell put that there? I most

definitely hadn't requested mistletoe. Then I spotted his clippers on the bottom step.

'You know you could have just aske—'

He closed the space between us, and I bit back my retort. That one step stole the breath right out of my lungs.

'You're so fucking beautiful,' he murmured, his voice warm enough to melt any resolve that might have lingered. Bracing one hand against the wall by my head, he used the other to cup my jaw, tracing his thumb over my cheek.

'Henry,' I breathed, unsure if it was a warning or a plea.

He leaned close enough that his breath tickled my ear, sending my pulse rocketing. I swallowed hard. My brain practically melted out of my ears. My muscles turned to stone as the heat from his body wrapped around me. All I could do was look up at him and wonder if he could hear my heartbeat echoing in my chest.

'Amanda,' he whispered, 'Wanting to be this close to you has plagued me for days.'

My knees nearly buckled.

I parted my lips to say something, but nothing came.

Absolutely nothing. Not one single sensible thought left. The fucker had emptied my brain.

The heat that rolled through me when he grazed his lower lip with his teeth was humiliating. You'd think I'd never had a hook-up before.

'Amanda.' Henry tipped my chin up a touch with his thumb. 'I don't need you to control things.'

My breath tangled with his as he tipped his face to mine.

'But I do need to kiss you right fucking now.'

My thoughts scattered as his lips pressed to mine. Not softly. Not sweetly. Like he'd been yearning for that one kiss.

The heat that tore straight through my spine amplified with each touch. His tight grip on my jaw, the other hand sliding down the wall and gathering my waist, pulling me flush against him. The kiss was slow but demanding, giving me no quarter but to let him lead.

And fuck me, I melted into a pile of wetness.

Pulling him closer, I fisted my hands in his jumper tightly enough for the material to bite into my skin. Heat curled low, building with each stroke of his tongue, his piney scent filling my every panted breath. I gave an embarrassingly needy little moan, and he swallowed it down like he was starving for it.

There was no teasing, no sunshine comments. Just his demanding mouth and the heat of his body pressed to mine. The soft sparkle of the nearby tree, which I hated a little less when being kissed halfway out of my own body.

Standing on my tiptoes, I gave in to the moment. Breathless and aching. Running my hands up over those deliciously veined arms.

When he eventually pulled back, I had to grip the wall to stay upright.

His forehead rested briefly against mine, his breath hot over my damp and swollen lips.

And then reality punched through my wanton haze.

Someone could walk in. A client could come down and find the gardener pinning me against the wall and snogging like a bloody teenager.

I slipped out from between him and the wall, straightening my top and tucking the escaped strands of my hair behind my ears.

'Right. That was. Well. Yes.' I stepped toward the stairs and felt heat fill my cheeks.

Henry's mouth twitched, amusement dancing in his eyes.

'Don't freak out, Amanda.'

'I'll see you in the morning,' I blurted out, turning

and making my escape up the stairs, praying I didn't slide on my ass in my haste. I didn't dare look back. If he gave me one more of those smouldering looks, I might forget every rule I'd ever made for myself.

My bedroom door clicked shut behind me, a barrier of safety between me and my goddamned horniness. Henry has unleashed my very tightly contained self and all I wanted was to go next door to his room and make him deal with what he'd done. But kissing him at work was bad enough; climbing into his bed would be a very stupid thing to do.

And I don't do stupid things.

No matter how much I desperately wanted to ride his stupid, happy fucking face.

So I did the next best thing.

Abandoned my underwear and grabbed my vibrator.

ten

OTTERLEIGH BAY VILLAGE NEWS
Late nights and phone lights

HENRY

Amanda's shut door stared at me. Daring me to knock.

She'd let her sensibility win, but before that she'd been a pile of sweet putty in my hands. And god, I needed more.

More of her hot little mouth.

More of her sweet sighs.

More of that lust-addled gaze when her lips were all swollen and pink.

I stood there in the hallway, breath still ragged from kissing her. Because fuck... that kiss had rocked me to my woollen socks.

But her very closed door was a no.

Sighing, I stumbled into my room. Into the emptiness and dark. My bed is neatly made up and not nearly as tempting as the one on the other side of the wall. Flopping down onto my bed, I let out a groan and rubbed my face, trying to figure out what the hell to do next.

And I heard something from beyond the wall.

A soft buzz, and an even softer moan.

Faint. Muffled. Delicious.

Amanda.

Another tiny, breathy moan like she'd tried to swallow it but couldn't.

I shifted on the bed, needing to adjust myself at the filthy little noise. Perhaps I'd left her at wound up as she'd left me.

An uppercut couldn't have wiped the grin off my face.

'Dirty girl,' I whispered into the darkness.

Tossing my pillows to the end of the bed, I lay as close to the wall as possible, greedily stealing each naughty little noise I could. Without even being in the same room, she had my dick straining.

I fumbled for my phone, cursing as it stuck in my pocket, my trousers suddenly far too tight. Before I could talk myself out of it, I sent her a text, thankful for her insistence that we all save her number before she arrived in case we, or she, needed anything.

> Sounds like I got you too excited...?

There was a pause next door, the buzzing ceasing.

It went on too long, and my stomach dropped.

I held my breath when the typing bubble appeared.

Then disappeared.

Appeared.

Disappeared.

> Did no one ever teach you it's rude to eavesdrop?

Fiesty.

This tightly-wound, prickly woman would be the death of me. I hadn't expected her to be teasing...

> Not my fault that I can hear every slutty little moan.

A moment later, the buzzing resumed, and a whimper followed, louder than before.

I closed my eyes, knuckles whitening around my phone.

> If you're going to eavesdrop, at least give me something to listen to.

My buttons worked against me in my haste to get my fucking trousers down. I groaned as I finally got my hand on myself, stroking over the head of my cock and letting out a groan.

I typed with one hand that barely functioned.

> You didn't strike me as a dirty girl...

The moan that filtered through the wall was anything but sweet. My strokes grew harsher with every delicious noise she gave.

> You have no idea.

The growl I let out was pure need. I wanted to burst through to her room and figure out exactly what she meant by that. The wall between us wasn't thick enough to keep our harried breath from combining, my jealousy growing with each buzz that filtered through. I'd have given my left ball to be between her thighs.

Her whimpers increased, and I closed my eyes, imagining myself there, tasting her, teasing her, making her squirm until she fell apart beneath my tongue. And my fingers. And my cock.

It didn't take long until her moaning changed, deepening until a delicious *Oh my god* came through the wall.

And straining to hear, maybe a whispered *Henry*, too. It might have been a figment of my imagination, a hope over reality, but it undid me anyway. My thighs tensed as I came hard, filling my hand with ropes of heat.

When I caught my breath, I took a photo of my hand, dripping for her, and prayed that she wouldn't use it against me.

> All for you.

I regretted it instantly.

Until her message popped up.

> Shame. If you had been here, I could have cleaned that up for you.

I dropped the phone and considered rushing through with my hand out for her.

My phone buzzed again.

> Sir.

Fuck me.

I dropped the phone on the bed and rubbed my face, getting myself a faceful of my own cum.

Damn. I stumbled to the bathroom and washed my face, laughing under my breath. That was a turn-up for the books. I hadn't imagined her like that.

Well, I had, but I hadn't expected it to be more than dirty thoughts of mine.

Maybe she'd be open to my games after all.

The idea sent a shiver down my spine. The good kind.

> Next time, I'll hold you to that, Princess.

Crashing back into bed, I fell asleep with my phone still in my hand, her admission bouncing around my head.

I woke to pale winter light creeping round the edges of the curtains, the kind of grey-white glow that threatened snow.

My phone lay on my pillow, still open on Amanda's messages.

I stared at the thread and felt that same heat I'd felt kissing her against the wall. Like someone had lit my boxers on fire. Or my lungs.

My body reacted by tightening and rising, desperate for her already.

'Fuck,' I muttered. How was I going to get through a day without pinning her somewhere and kissing her until she called me Sir for real?

Sleep hadn't fixed anything. I'd woken up even more obsessed with the woman I barely knew. More unsure of what the hell to do next.

I showered and dressed before stepping out into the corridor. Her door remained shut. Checking my phone, I loitered in the hall.

Then I heard movement and stilled, listening again.

Until her door opened and I tried, and presumably failed, to look nonchalant.

Amanda stepped out looking like the previous night had never happened. Hair smoothed back into a neat ponytail, dress ironed to perfection, not a wrinkle out of place. Not a single trace of what had passed between us.

She blinked at me before heading down the corner, leaving me to follow like a trained puppy.

'Morning,' I said.

She didn't fumble.

Didn't even hesitate.

'We've a full schedule today,' she said lightly. Professionally. 'The florists will need access to the orangery at eight. Catering is delivering fresh supplies at nine. And I'll need those boxes of spare linens brought in from storage.'

A flare of need spiked. The need to pin her down and demand her full attention. To tame this side of her with my tongue. But not for too long. I *liked* her like this. It made me crave her giving in all the more.

'Amanda,' I said quietly.

She slowed. *Barely*. Turning just enough to look over her shoulder.

'Yes?'

'About last night—' I began.

She cut me off. 'Henry, I'm at work'

Work.

'Of course,' I said, trying to stop the disappointment from hitting my face.

She continued down the corridor, shoulders tight. I followed slowly, keeping distance. Watching the way she moved, like she had armour on. A slight tremble in her fingers was the only tell that she was even slightly affected by the previous night.

Amanda stood by the coffee machine in the

kitchen, and I leaned on the counter, watching her. She stared very pointedly at her clipboard.

Finally, she spoke.

'I don't have time for complications,' she said.

Complications.

As if what happened last night hadn't rocked her the way it rocked me. Maybe it hadn't. Maybe I was just a *blip*.

'I didn't think it was complicated, I thought it was hot.'

The way her pupils dilated gave her away, and I couldn't help but grin. But she recovered instantly, her jaw tightening.

'I need to go,' she said, already moving.

I stared after her. She could pretend it didn't happen. But I'd heard her moans. Seen the messages. Got a glimpse of the woman beneath the pristine exterior. And I wanted more.

Needed more.

And if the rest of the week kept going like that, I wasn't sure either of us would make it to Christmas without exploding.

eleven

> OTTERLEIGH BAY VILLAGE NEWS
>
> The Bayview Manor Orangery's windows are looking extra steamy. Cold shower, anyone?

AMANDA

I HAD SPENT HALF THE DAY PRETENDING I WASN'T AVOIDING Henry, which I failed at constantly. Whenever he was in the same room as me, I couldn't keep my eyes off him. He was attractive enough when he was bounding about all smiles, but the brooding energy that rolled off of him was tantalising. It hit a part of me that I'd left wanting far too long.

And yet one single night of, well, barely even phone sex, had me sneaking looks at him like a lust-drunk idiot.

By mid-afternoon, Henry went AWOL. And

although I resisted the urge to hunt him down for a solid forty-five minutes to catch a glimpse, I found myself heading into the warm humidity of the orangery. Not the fancy one many older mansions had, but one that breathed on its own, with tropical plants wedged in every corner.

And one Henry James.

The thick air made my chest ache as I stepped inside. Condensation dripped, marking a soft beat as I made my way through the jungle of plants.

Henry stood near the centre, tall rose bushes framing him, shirt sleeves rolled up, and a sheen of sweat glistening on his throat. The late winter sun threw golden highlights over him, like a Renaissance-painted angel. But under those sweet blond curls, he wasn't cherubic at all. I'd seen beyond his curtain of cheer, and something altogether more delicious lurked there. Something potentially worth risking my reputation for.

Maybe.

I lingered in the doorway, both unsure about approaching him and riveted at watching him work. Stepping forward, the door clicked behind me. His gaze snapped to me, and I stilled.

'Amanda.'

Had his voice always been so damned throaty?

When he said my name like that, I wanted nothing more than to throw myself at him. But I held back. He quirked a brow when I froze, before placing his snips on the rough wooden worktop.

'Come here.'

The demand forced my feet forward, every step closer, sending my pulse rocketing in my throat until it sounded almost as loud in my ears as the dripping condensation.

'I wanted to apologise about this morning. I didn't mean to blow you off. Well, I did. But I might be regretting it.'

He folded his arms, the muscles bunching.

'It's alright.'

'I admitted something that I wanted to take back, but that's obviously impossible.'

His eyes darkened.

'When you offered to lick up my mess, or when you called me Sir?' There was no malice in the question, but it still made me squirm.

Heat ricocheted through me as I stopped in front of him, his eyes sweeping over me and leaving me feeling utterly exposed.

'I didn't say I'd lick it up.'

'No.' He stepped toward me, rounding until I was between him and the worktop. 'But that's what you meant. And now you're ashamed for letting me know about that fantasy of yours. What you're missing is how I knew exactly what you meant without you saying it. I think we are cut from the same cloth, Amanda.'

I should have left.

Shoulda, coulda, woulda.

Instead, I leaned back on the table, letting my dress hitch up just enough to show a flash of thigh.

When he moved forward, pressing momentarily against me, I readied myself for another soul-snatching kiss. Fuck, he could kiss for Britain. I'd had his damn mouth on my mind all day, and I was so ready for another taste, no matter how reckless. Instead, he reached past me, lifting a rose he'd cut earlier. It was deep crimson, long-stemmed and studded with thorns.

A sweet gesture, but not what I'd come for.

'Sit on the worktop,' he commanded. 'And open your legs.'

What the heck? I hoped to god he didn't think he'd be using me as a damned vase. I was kinky, but not thorns in the chuff kinky.

Before I could formulate my argument, Henry leaned in and brushed his lips against my throat.

'Trust me.'

Two little words that challenged me. Could I trust him? This near stranger who enchanted donkeys and Australians with nought but a sunny smile. Who mistletoe trapped me?

My body obeyed before my brain did. He guided me backwards and lifted me until I sat on the table top, the rough wood digging into my backside through my dress.

'You're trembling.' He ran a thumb over my lip.

'I can't help it.' I hated how bloody breathy he made me.

'Good.'

Henry tipped the rose and grazed the petals over my exposed thigh.

Cool silk against my sticky skin. I watched as the red contrasted with my thigh, dancing over my flesh and sending ripples of sensation through me.

'This is where it begins, you focus on what I let you feel, and you let everything else fall away. There's just you, me, and this rose.

He dragged the petal slowly upwards as my eyes fluttered closed. I couldn't help but sigh as the petals neared the apex of my thighs, barely covered by the hem of my dress.

Then a thorn grazed the same path. Replacing the

soft sensation with a much more acute one. Not breaking skin, but sharp enough to make me flinch.

'And this heightens the sensations. It takes all that pleasure and tightens it, rolling it into something far deeper.'

I quaked as need washed over me. It was mortifying how he made me ache with nothing but a flower.

He tilted my chin sharply with his free hand. 'Do you know why I love roses so much?'

'Everyone likes roses.'

'No,' Henry said. 'Everyone is told they love roses. Because they are pretty. But that's not what I love about roses. I love that they have contrast. So sharp that they can draw blood, yet so soft they can make even the prettiest, most tightly controlled woman whimper.'

Henry flipped the rose again, making me moan as he tauted me with the velvety flower, dancing it over the crotch of my panties.

'Too soft,' I begged.

'So demanding.' Henry didn't give more; he kept me there, on the table, arching toward him in desperation.

'You are just like the roses, Amanda. All spikey if you don't approach with care, but beneath it all, you're just as delicate as the petals. When you let me past the sharpness, the rewards will be oh so sweet.'

'Maybe I'm all thorns,' I muttered, tipping my head back as the thorns grazed over my panties.

'Not with me.' He lifted the rose higher, dragging it over my cheek.

The bloom slid down my throat, over my collarbone, down to my chest, snagging in the fabric of my dress.

'Henry...'

'Look at me.'

I did. The heat burning in his eyes had me pressing my thighs together and a flush rushing to my face.

'If I were to take this further,' he said, delicately feeling a scratch the thorn had left on my thigh, 'I'd have you focus on my voice. My touch. Nothing else. No guilt. No professionalism. No overthinking.'

Then he kissed me.

Soft. Far too soft. I needed him to lose control, to follow me down into the pit of lust that he'd launched me into.

I gripped his shirt to steady myself. To demand more.

He broke the kiss, his voice rough. 'Not here. Not now. I want nothing more than to discover every single way I can make you plead. But I'm also here to protect you. And fucking you in a room full of windows mid-day wouldn't be in your best interest. No matter how fucking hard you have me.'

I was on the verge of begging. I knew I was. There was no stopping it.

'Amanda. Are you in here?'

Rita.

I jerked like I'd been clocked in the arse with a taser.

Henry winced, then stepped back just far enough for cool air to rush between us.

Fucking terrible timing, Rita.

'Go,' he murmured. 'Before she comes in and finds you wet and me rocking a tent.'

There was no way my face wasn't puce.

It took me a moment to steady myself when he lifted me to the floor, my ability to walk having fled with my senses.

twelve

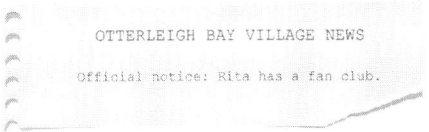

OTTERLEIGH BAY VILLAGE NEWS
Official notice: Rita has a fan club.

HENRY

By the time I closed up the orangery, the estate had gone quiet. Likely having their evening meal in the elaborate dining room. A blanket of frost descended on the manor, and I groaned. I'd need to resalt the steps and paths before I could go and find Amanda.

She'd plagued my mind since the moment I woke up, and only increased my obsession with her midday rose-filled visit. God only knew how she'd react to my little game, but her response had filled me with hope. Hope that she would let me behind her walls. Hope that I could see more of her smiles.

I just found my eyes drifting toward her window as I crossed the garden, eager for the slightest glimpse of her.

Nothing.

Following the path to the salt box, I started shovelling gritty salt into a wheelbarrow.

A hat bobbed on the other side of the wall.

'Evening,' I shouted.

Lisa popped her head up, her blonde hair sticking out from her head in wild strands. Her cheeks were as pink as her nose in the frostbitten air.

'You've got a face on you tonight.' She tipped her head.

'I'm not sure even I can be smiley when shovelling.'

'At least it's salt and not Merv's leftovers today.'

'True.'

I rubbed a cold hand over my jaw and put down my shovel for a moment. 'I like the event planner.'

Lisa grinned. '*Like her*, like her?'

'Big time.'

'And that makes you...sad?'

'No. I'm just trying to figure out how to get closer to her. She's a bit guarded.'

Lisa considered my words for a moment. 'Some

people are like that because it's how they were taught to cope. Doesn't mean they want to be.'

'Have you tried inviting her out for something fun? Something that's not cooped up in the manor? You men always make things harder than they need to be. The quiz is on at the pub tonight, right?'

'Yeah.'

'Take her. Let her see you in a less pressured environment. If you're stressing, she'll be stressing.'

'You make it sound easy.'

'That's because it is,' she said.

Maybe Lisa had a point. The worst Amanda could do was say no. 'I'll ask her.'

'Good. And maybe try a shower and a real shirt. You don't always need to look like you're about to dig up the garden.'

It wasn't as easy as Lisa had said it would be.

Inviting Amanda to the quiz led all the adult clients to decide to come too. So rather than a quiet night away from her clients, I'd managed to gift Amanda a night with them in a roasting local pub rather than an expansive manor house.

By the time we got to the Tipsy Otter, the place was already packed. Half the village had crammed in, coats over the backs of chairs, cheeks red from the cold and the clink of glasses filling the air. The smell of mulled cider filled the air with notes of cinnamon and apple.

The Petersens walked in ahead of us in a gaggle of excitement. You'd think they'd entered Narnia rather than a pub in Scotland. Just about every little detail thrilled them.

Amanda hovered like a sheepdog. Circling them with antsy attention.

'It's so cute,' Rita said, clutching her scarf even though it was roasting indoors.

'It's certainly busy,' Bill, Rita's son, added.

'I'm sure you'll have a fab time,' Amanda said, her face not nearly as convincing as her tone. She got the nine Australians settled at a far too small table near the bar before hovering nearby.

'Relax,' I said, fighting the urge to wrap my arms around her waist. 'They'll have fu.'

'They might hate it.'

'Who hates a quiz night? Look at them, do they look like they are hating it?'

She didn't look convinced.

Jean Harris spotted us and waved madly. I smiled. As much as I was fond of the residents of Otterleigh Bay, Jean was my favourite. She reminded me of my grandmother, and regularly welcomed me into her home for a cup of tea and a natter. 'We have two spare seats, come on over.'

Amanda looked ready to protest when I guided her over. 'What about the Petersens?'

'They've managed to build a multimillion-pound company, I'm sure they'll cope with some beer and questions.'

Everyone shifted to make room: Jean and Jim slid down the bench, Claire and Owen moved a whole pile of coats. I slid in beside Amanda, quite pleased at the lack of space. It gave the perfect excuse to have her pressed up against me.

'You alright?' I whispered.

'Yes.' She took a large swig of her chilled white wine and swallowed hard.

The quiz started with a riotous cheer and the scratch of cheap biros on hard tables.

Kenny shouted something about no cheating when a sullen-looking boy of nineteen or so scrolled through his phone. He rolled his eyes and put it on the table while the other tables heckled him jovially.

The quiz continued, question after question through a mix of laughter, chatter and hearty competition. Amanda was doing her best beside me, but she remained stiff beside me. She smiled at the right moments, nodded politely when the Harrised spoke to her, and even got a round in.

But every few minutes, she gave me a look. A flicker of concern before her eyes flicked to her clients.

'You're overthinking,' I whispered when she stiffened beside me yet again.

'No I'm not.'

'Liar.'

The Petersens, meanwhile, were having a whale of a time.

They were laughing harder than I'd seen all day, already making firm friends with a load of the locals. Morag in particular, along with he dog Scruff, seemed taken with Rita. Scruff sat in her lap, oblivious to the dog hair that covered her expensive sweater. Not that Rita seemed to care. She patted him rhythmically, like a furry little drum.

But Amanda watched them as if they were toddlers who'd just discovered walking.

At one point, Bill got up to buy another drink, and she jolted as though to follow him.

I touched her wrist before she fully stood.

'Amanda, they're fine, I promise.'

Her eyes narrowed, those spikes rising. Then she slowly sat back down. Her pulse beat fast as I held her, the little thump quickening beneath my fingertips.

The quiz eventually ended in a tie-break between the Petersens and a local family. In the end, the locals won. Not that the Petersens seemed to mind one iota. They'd already drained Kenny's small selection of not-very-nice champagne and moved onto the top shelf whiskies. Not only for them, but they also purchased by the bottle and quite liberally topped everyone up around them.

Claire smiled softly at Owen, before turning to Amanda.

'I heard that you made Bayview look outstanding. Word is that you're like a Christmas magician.'

I choked on my drink.

Amanda flushed. 'Well, I'm not sure about that. In the end, the kids decorated it with Henry here, in just about every shade under the sun.'

'I saw some pictures that Eilidh saw from Emmy, who saw them from one of the waitresses. I love your style. The glass, the gold touches, the soft lighting and real evergreens. Perfection.'

A smile lit up Amanda's face, and she finally really relaxed, leaning her side against mine.

And then someone ordered shots.

A lot of shots.

And the Petersens looked guilty of the crime. I passed, but to my surprise, Amanda took one of the little red glasses and clinked it with Claire's before downing it and coughing.

'Christ,' she said, taking a sip of wine and wincing again. 'What is that?'

'Only Kenny knows. I think he calls it a Christmas Warmer. Probably all the leftover bottles mixed.'

'It tastes like paint stripper.' Amanda scrunched her nose.

'You'll get used to it eventually,' Claire laughed.

'Oh, I'm only here until the twenty-eighth, so it'll thankfully be a one-time occurrence.'

The sting that bit me when she said that took great care to hide. It was a reminder that whatever was going on between us was just a fling. If that. When I already wanted so much more.

Rita, at her ripe age of eighty-three, downed hers like it was cordial.

Claire's sister-in-law, Isla, shouted, 'That's the spirit!'

Amanda groaned. 'I'm going to have to find at least six sick buckets when we get back.'

'At least they're enjoying it,' I said, letting my hand drape behind her.

'That's true.' She blinked up at me, those dark eyes glittering with the reflected fairy lights above us.

And then, from the corner of my eye, I saw Isla head for the bar, grabbing her friend Eilidh on the way. Then, grabbing Rita.

'Rita!' she shrieked. 'Come dance.'

Before either of us could intervene, Rita, Eilidh and Isla clambered onto the bar.

All of them giggled as they looked down at us. Someone wolf-whistled, and the pub erupted as the jukebox kicked in. The three women started dancing tipsily, as multiple others stood below them, looking ready to catch them from the inevitable fall.

And then they started dancing.

Full *Coyote Ugly* style.

Tinsel yanked from the ceiling as boas. A bowl of crisps kicked into a lap.

Amanda jolted upright.

'Oh my God. Rita, get down! Rita!'

I caught her forearm as she rose, and eased her back into her seat.

'Breathe,' I said quietly.

'Henry—'

'They're fine.'

'They're on the bar.'

'And?'

'*And?!*'

'They're adults. They can bar dance until Kenny kicks them out.'

She glanced at the bar where Rita was absolutely living her best life, Isla laughing so hard she was clutching her stomach, Eilidh flicking fairy lights like a lasso. Then she looked at the Petersens, who looked delighted by the carnage.

'My insurance absolutely doesn't cover bar dancing,' she said at last.

'They're having a proper Scottish party.' I nudged her shoulder. 'And you can't ruin it by policing their fun.'

She exhaled slowly and let her hand rest on my thigh, which sent my brain melting out of my ears.

'Maybe I am a bit tightly wound,' Amanda admitted.

'A bit,' I said. 'But it's alright. I can think of half a dozen ways to help you unwind.'

Her eyes snapped to mine, and for a moment, the noise around us ceased to matter.

Just us.

Then Rita dropped a shot glass into someone's pint, and the spell shattered.

Amanda groaned, but stayed seated, her fingers drawing tiny circles on my thigh. She leaned back against my arm, letting the chaos continue around her.

thirteen

> OTTERLEIGH BAY VILLAGE NEWS
> An exasperated groan heard in Otterleigh Bay.
> Seems like frustrations are high on the hill.

AMANDA

BY LATE MORNING, REINDEER FILLED THE DRIVEWAY, AS well as half of the village. What had been arranged as a photoshoot with the elaborately decorated sleigh, a very realistic Father Christmas, and a whole team of antlered reindeer had turned into an impromptu gathering. After many drinks, Rita had suggested that anyone with kids come on up. The photographer had been somewhat dismayed until I negotiated a fat cheque for her. Rita hadn't even blinked, just added a couple of zeros and signed it off. The children were bouncing like they'd had sugar-coated syrup-laden E-numbers for breakfast.

The housekeeper, Pru, fussed over them with glee.

Which meant I had a chance to step away.

To relax my aching false smile and breathe away from the rather smelly animals.

And perhaps to find Henry. Like it or not, he kept invading my brain. The memory of his warm hand on my spine, steady and safe. That million-watt smile, which had gone from annoying to me, to filling me with butterflies.

The moment I spotted the orangery, something reached low inside me and tugged me toward it. Before I'd thought twice, my boots were crunching across the frosty gravel, my stomach flip-flopping with nerves. And excitement.

The greenhouse was thick with the scent of damp earth and the faint sweetness of whatever winter blooms Henry grew. Low light caught on leaves and cast diffused shadows on the red brick floor, and amongst all the foliage knelt Henry, snipping at forest green boughs and strapping them to willow strips that had been melded into a circle. Completed wreaths balanced around him, filled with deep red berries, pinecones and frosted-looking, furred leaves.

He didn't glance up.

'Good morning, Amanda.'

There were enough people in the manor that I wondered how he'd known it was me.

'How did you know it was me?'

Henry's eyes finally met mine, a smile lifting the corner of his mouth.

'Your scent.'

I froze by the door. What did he mean by that? My perfume? I was pretty sure I didn't stink.

'What?'

'I can tell when you're in the room, or have just left a room. It's a mixture of cocoa butter, the floral smell of your perfume, vanilla and rose, and underneath it all, the enchanting scent of you.'

Well. Fuck. He knew my scent. He acted like a golden retriever, but I didn't expect him to have the nose of a bloodhound, too.

'Do you tend to go around sniffing people?'

'I can't say I've ever noticed someone's scent before. But I can't help but notice you, Amanda.'

The butterflies turned into great flapping seagulls in my stomach.

'So, what can I do for you?' The question hung in the space between us.

I had a few suggestions. Kiss me until I can't

breathe. Bend me over the workbench. Put me on my knees and...'

I swallowed, trying to steady myself. 'I was checking if you needed anything before you head off to the Christmas market.'

He tied off some twine before beckoning me to him.

His expression was infuriatingly unreadable.

'Try again.'

The words slid under my ribs and sent my heartbeat thundering.

Heat rose to my cheeks at the simple demand. I didn't need to pretend I was there under some ploy. Henry made it clear that it's okay to let my guard down. That it's okay to want.

'I want...' Knowing it was okay to tell him didn't make it any easier to do so. 'You to kiss me.'

Henry's expression changed, his pleasure marking his grin, and those blue eyes darkened like a stormy sea.

Standing, he said, 'Come here.'

I obeyed, crossing the room, my pulse quickening when I stood before him, looking up into that devilishly sweet face. His eyes flicked to my mouth as I wet my lips. When his fingers brushed the side of my jaw, I inhaled sharply, the smallest of his touches lighting me up brighter than the monstrous Christmas tree inside.

'I haven't stopped thinking about these damned lips,' he murmured, almost to himself. 'Or the way you whimper into my mouth. The way your breath catches when I touch you...' His thumb traced lightly along my lower lip. 'It's the prettiest thing I've ever heard.'

The words hit like a physical sensation, darting straight between my thighs and spreading heat through me.

'Here?'

'Anywhere,' he said. '*Everywhere.*'

The *everywhere* was positively salacious.

Tipping my jaw, his lips brushed the side of my neck in a slow kiss that sent sparks through me in an unbroken wave. His breath skimmed my skin, and the soft touch unravelled all the tightness I'd been holding in my chest.

He kissed just below my ear next, lingering on my pulse point as I placed my hands on his thick chest, feeling the solidity of him. Then he found my mouth and kissed me with unhurried depth, erasing any thoughts of reindeer, photographers, clients and the outside world.

The stroke of his tongue practically wiped my

name from my head. I curled my fingers into his woollen jumper, demanding more with the eagerness of my own mouth.

Then footsteps crunched on the path outside the glass.

A male voice, one of the Petersens, calling my name. I flinched, pulling back from the kiss and seeing red. I just wanted five god damned minutes to lose myself in Henry's mouth. Was that too much to ask?

'Henry, someone's coming.'

He didn't push me away. Instead, he pulled me deeper into the foliage, placing himself between me and a wooden table.

Then he sank to his knees.

Right at my feet.

Right between my thighs.

'What are you doing?' I asked through gritted teeth as Bill Petersen came into the orangery.

He didn't answer. His fingers wrapped around my black leggings and tugged me closer to him, settling himself where the potting bench and the angle of the worktable hid him from sight.

'Ah, Amanda,' Mr Petersen called as he stepped inside. 'Sorry to interrupt. Just wanted to check when we'll be doing the next round of photos, the kids are…'

I forced my attention to Bill, trying to ignore the warmth of Henry's breath brushing the inside of my thigh through the fabric of my trousers.

'Yes, of course.' I aimed for a professional tone, but it came out far too high-pitched. 'I'll be with you in just a few moments.'

Henry's hands slid around my arse, tugging me against his face. The grazing of his thumbs over my hips had me reaching forward to grip the table.

I all but forgot how to speak as he slowly kissed my thighs, grazing over the front of my trousers as he alternated sides. Mr Petersen kept talking, blissfully oblivious of the sinner beneath the table, explaining something about how one of the kids had her hat eaten by one of the reindeer.

I nodded along, hoping he didn't hear the squeak I gave when Henry kissed me right *there*. Heat engulfed me between the thighs as I saw stars. It had been far, far too long since I'd had someone there. If only he'd yank down my trousers and let me feel his tongue.

'You alright there?' Bill asked.

'God, yes,' I sighed, before catching the throaty way I said it. 'I mean, yes. Thank you. I'll be with you in a moment.'

Henry's fingers stroked higher, arching my hips to give his mouth more access to me. His lips teased through the material. The fact that he didn't stop when someone came in sent mixed signals to my body. I should push him off. Tell him to stop. But it only heightened my need. Made tingles sweep through me.

Mercifully, Mr Petersen excused himself and left the orangery. I braced a hand on the edge of the workbench, trying to find some words.

'Henry, what the hell do you think you're doing?'

He rose slowly, his hands skimming the entirety of my rear as he did. When he finally stood in front of me again, he spun us around, pinning me against the bench, pure hunger marking his face. Being caged by him only had me all the more desperate for more of his delicious touch.

'What I'm doing,' he said, his voice deep and gravelly, 'is giving you exactly what you came looking for. You asked me to kiss you. You didn't say where.'

'You can't just do that sort of thing.'

'Yes, I can.' He slid a hand into my hair before tightening his grip, painfully tipping my face to his. The ache took my breath away, the heady mixture of pain and pleasure sharpening the lust pooling between my thighs. 'Because you want it. Don't you?'

You bet your sweet arse I did.

Then he kissed me again, an all-consuming collision that stole any doubt straight out of my lungs and replaced it with heat so sharp it ached. My fingers grasped at him, hunting for something to hold onto, and when he pressed forward, I felt an unmistakable hardness against me. Losing any sense of shame, I ground my hips, moaning at the curls of pleasure the pressure against my leggings elicited.

'Henry,' I breathed.

He rested his forehead against mine for a second before pulling back, his fingers still lost in my hair.

'Later,' he said, rougher than before. 'I want nothing more than to let you grind your sweet cunt against me until you lose all that pent-up control, but you've got clients waiting, and I have a market to attend.'

It took a full three seconds for the words to make sense.

'No... I need this.'

'I know you do, and I'll gladly sink between those thighs until you scream the fucking manor down, but the wait will make it all the more satisfying.'

'You can't leave me like this.'

He stepped back and smiled. 'Oh, but I can.'

'Maybe I'll just go find my vibrator.'

'If you think it'll satisfy the itch, Princess. But I have a feeling it'll only leave you needing more.

There's only so much silicone can do. It can't make you pant like I just did, can it? It can balance pain and pleasure until your brain malfunctions. But by all means... If you can't wait for me.'

That smug arsehole.

And the worst part? He was right. I didn't want a quick fix. I wanted him to finish what he started.

'Bring the Petersens down to the market after lunch. I'll be waiting for you.'

I left the greenhouse with heat flushing from my face to, well, far lower, and my legs akin to Bambi's.

Wetter. Hornier. *Angrier.*

Because I wasn't used to letting someone else lead. As much as he made me weak at the knees, I also wanted to just pin him down and take what I needed, so I could get it out of my head.

Get *him* out of my head.

fourteen

OTTERLEIGH BAY VILLAGE NEWS
Two old birds and a donkey dressed as a camel spotted at the Christmas market.

AMANDA

OTTERLEIGH BAY VILLAGE SQUARE WAS BURSTING AT THE seams with chaos.

Christmas hat-laden children with runny noses performed in a nativity on a central stage, while all around, people bustled from market stall to market stall, laughing and chatting and purchasing treats. String lights criss-crossed from one building to another, while the sheen of frost made it look straight off a Christmas card.

There was no denying that it was a picturesque place. And that the people who lived there were friendly. The place practically dripped with community spirit. Heck, even Merv was invited.

The Petersens had descended in mass, oohing and aahing over every charming little detail. The children were crowding around Merv's pen beside the nativity, while their parents were truly putting their spending power to use. There would be a lot of very happy crafters come dinner time. Bill bought a scarf so long it could outdo Dr Who's one, and his adult son, Elijah, carried two steaming mugs of spiced cider and three bursting bags of fudge while his husband tried to convince their son he didn't need a six-foot willow reindeer sculpture. I'd followed along behind Rita for a while, until it became perfectly obvious that she didn't need my assistance.

Children screeching by the bandstand, clambering over tartan-blanketed hay bales while worrying mothers adjusted the angel's wings and wiped the shepherds' runny noses.

Merv happily munched on a carrot offered to him by the child narrator of the nativity, looking pleased with himself. They'd draped him in a fleece blanket with two humps that looked very pillow-shaped on his back. Despite there very much being a donkey in the nativity story, Merv appeared to have been cast as a camel. Not that he seemed to mind one bit.

All went suspiciously well until halfway through a high-pitched rendition of Away in a Manger, when Merv decided the set was tastier than the carrots. First, he plucked a shepherd's hat, a tea towel with a band of elastic, clean off of a boy's head. Then he pushed the side of his pen over and took the steps up to the low stage, tucking in to the manger hay after having yeeted the plastic baby Jesus into the audience.

Mary was beside herself, tears streaming down her face as the teachers tried to coax Merv back into his pen. Joseph, however, took to pulling handfuls of hay from the bales and hand feeding Merv, looking utterly delighted with the chaotic turn of events.

Parents filmed the nativity and laughed, most likely having sat through endless nativities and having never seen one go quite so sideways so fast. Henry eventually left his wreaths to go save the day, encouraging Merv off the stage and back into the pen, holding him there quite firmly as the teachers tried to restore order on stage.

A glassblower's stall caught my eye, the intricate ornaments glittering in the low sun. I made my way over, charmed by the colourful tree decorations, each utterly unique. Sweaty golden angels with halos so impossibly thin. A family of spotted deer.

Red-breasted robins. But one in particular made me stop.

A glass donkey, just like Merv. Albeit better behaved. With spindly legs and the sweetest nose, and tall ears, a ribbon fastened to his back to hang him on a tree. Imperfection shaped his face, the nose a little short, and the eyes not perfectly matched, but it only added to its quaintness.

Would it be crazy to buy it for Henry?

It's not like we were... well, anything really. Other than both horny and single. Gift buying felt a little premature.

He kissed you between your thighs not three hours ago.

I supposed a little gift wouldn't hurt.

Before I could talk myself out of it, I passed over a twenty-pound note and accepted a striped gold bag. I carefully tucked it into the pocket of my coat, glad of the box the seller had secured it in. I could decide whether to hand it over later. If all else failed, I guessed I'd have a glass donkey to find a home for. Or a little memory of my one Christmas in Otterleigh Bay.

'Amanda,' Owen Harris, the local whisky distiller, beckoned me to his stall and offered me a plastic shot glass of amber liquid. 'Bottoms up.'

He looked like a tourist's wet dream. Clad in a kilt

and cosy jumper, and surrounded by booze. His fiancée, Claire, stood with her arm wrapped around his waist, her nose pink and her cheeks pinker.

'It helps with the cold,' she said, taking a shot for herself.

'I'm still working.' I swirled the whisky in the glass and took a sniff.

'I'm not sure your clients will mind,' Owen replied, reaching for a tiny glass. 'Rita's already visited us three times, and I'm quite sure we'll be sending a barrel up the road to the manor if she comes back again.'

With a shrug, I gave in and took a sip.

The whisky hit my tongue and heat shot down my throat, so intense and unexpected that my eyes began to water.

'Bloody hell, that's potent.'

Claire clapped with glee.

'Oh my God, if you could see your face right now.'

I coughed, willing my eyes to stop streaming. 'Why is it so fiery?'

'You need a strong whisky in this weather,' Owen grinned.

'You get used to it,' Claire added.

Owen bent to kiss the top of her head, their easy relationship making my chest knot unexpectedly. I hadn't been a lot of happy relationships. They seemed so comfortable with one another. And the soft way Owen looked at Claire practically melted me.

Claire gave a sly smile.

'Tell me, since your soul momentarily left your body, did a certain strapping gardener feature in the flashbacks?'

'I don't know what you're talking about.' My cheeks flamed, and I hoped I could blame it on the alcohol.

'Mmm-hm. I don't suppose you've noticed the curly-haired Adonis loitering around the manor at all. You know, the one you were pressed up against in the pub...' Owen gave Claire a nudge and told her to behave.

Morag and Jean appeared like guardian angels and swept me away from the whisky stall.

Morag looped her arm through mine as though we were old friends and not almost-strangers. And I had to admit, it didn't feel totally terrible.

'There you are,' Morag said warmly. 'And look how much you're glowing.'

'I am not glowing,' I protested.

'You are,' Jean said, matter-of-factly. 'And we all know why.'

'It's just the whisky.'

Morag snorted. 'It's okay to have noticed our Henry, you know. He's a good boy.'

I hoped not.

'He's just a colleague. I barely know him.' The two older women exchanged a look. 'It's only been a few days.'

'A few days can be plenty,' Jean said with a knowing nod.

'When it's right, it doesn't take long at all,' Morag added. 'My Alistair knew within a day.'

'This is very kind, but I think you've gotten the wrong end of the stick.' Because I hadn't even got the end of his stick yet. And they were both talking like I'd met my husband.

Without meaning to, I found Henry in the crowd. He crouched beside a little girl who held a rankly gargantuan wreath and was fixing a pink ribbon to the front while she bounced with excitement. There was a softness to him around children and animals that contrasted sharply with the side of him that he'd given me glimpses of.

As if he could feel my gaze, he looked over.

The faintest smile tipped his mouth, and I remembered his time on his knees earlier in the day.

Nope.

Do not go there.

Morag followed my gaze and patted my arm.

'Sometimes… that's all it takes,' she murmured.

And the biggest problem was that she might be right.

I'd lost my mind and started fantasising over a man I'd only be around for a few days.

```
OTTERLEIGH BAY VILLAGE NEWS
A stitch in time says mine.
```

HENRY

After securing Merv back into his stable, with a slight reprimand for showing me up, I headed back to the village and straight for Jean's cottage. The older woman and I had formed a happy friendship over the few years I had been in Otterleigh Bay. She was kind and sweet, and she made truly excellent biscuits. I helped her and her husband, Jim, with the jobs she'd banned him from doing. It was a perfectly symbiotic relationship.

She also made for a fantastic sounding board when I needed one.

A rush of warmth hit me when she opened the door and ushered me in out of the cold, dark evening.

'I didn't think I'd be seeing you today,' she said, taking my coat from me and hanging it on the end of the bannister. 'Jim's popped over to Islas's to fuss over the wee one. He's smitten now that there are smiles to be won.'

'Couldn't leave my favourite girl hanging.'

Jean grinned and slapped my arm before shooing me into the kitchen.

'Are you sure I'm still your favourite?' She put on the kettle while I took a seat, going straight for one of the homemade custard creams. The biscuit melted on my tongue, and I couldn't help but groan.

'With bakes like these? You might still have the lead.'

Jean couldn't help but preen at the praise, and I loved making her feel appreciated. 'Your face says otherwise.'

'My face?'

'Mmm. You've the face of a man with a woman on his mind.'

How she could see that on my face, I wasn't sure. Maybe it was the sort of things old ladies said to cover the tracks of gleeful gossip.

She took a seat opposite me, and poured the tea,

handing me a steaming cup and looking at the folded-over plastic bag I'd set on the table. The way she looked at it told me she itched to ask what was inside.

'Thank you,' I said as she pushed my mug of tea over. 'I hope you don't mind if I ask for a bit of help?'

'It's rare I can help you with much other than a plate of biscuits, I'd be delighted if there's something I can do.'

I slipped a Christmas jumper out of my bag and set it on the table. The very same one Jean had made for me two Christmases ago when I'd spent Christmas with the Harrises.

A deep green wool jumper with a huge H embroidered on it in thick, glittering thread.

Jean looked at the folded jumper, reaching out to dance her wrinkled fingers over the hem. 'I recognise this. Have you grown sick of it?'

'No. Not at all. I just think someone else might need it more than I do.'

'Amanda? I'm not sure it's quite her style, or fit.'

'It's less the jumper and more what it represents. It made me feel at home when you included me in your tradition, and I want her to feel a little bit of that Christmas magic, too. She said that her family never really did any traditions, so I thought I might gift her one.'

'Is she changing her name to Hamanda?' There was a wicked glint in Jean's eyes that had me laughing.

'I doubt it very much. I was hoping you still had some of this gold thread and could show me how to turn the H into an A.'

Jean leaned forward and nodded.

'An A,' she repeated. 'Aye. We can do that for your girl.'

I opened my mouth to insist that she wasn't *mine*, yet, but Jean's hand shot out before I could.

'Don't go lying to me, Henry James, you want the letter changed because the lass means something to you.'

I felt heat creep up my neck.

'I've known her for four days. *Four.*'

'And since when has that ever mattered?' Jean tutted. 'Jim told me he was going to marry me on our first date. I thought he'd lost his mind. And married him anyway.'

'You've told me this story before.'

'And I'll tell you a dozen more times until you get it into your noggin that time is irrelevant.'

Shaking her head at me, she fetched the thick

golden threat and a fat needle, looping them together and signalling for me to hand the jumper over.

'Can I help?' I asked.

Jean looked up at me and smiled. 'It'll be quicker if I do it.'

'But it'll mean more if I help.'

Her eyes misted as she nodded. 'Well, you'd best put on a pot of tea, lad. We'll be here a while.'

It took a few tries for me to figure out the stitch she used to make the thick, raised lettering, but within half an hour, I figured it out, and painstakingly worked to make my stitches just as neat as Jean's as I closed the top of the H.

'You'll be home for a bit after Christmas?'

'Yeah, for a few days,' I said.

'Will you be back for Hogmanay?'

'I'm not sure. Depends on what the Leadbetters need. And whether—'

'You'll need to be back. Because Owen and Claire are surprising everyone with a wedding at the ceilidh.'

I dropped the needle and stared at her.

'*A wedding?*'

Jean nodded.

'They're getting married. In a week?'

'Decided it yesterday. We're keeping it quiet. They

want it small and without a fuss. Just cosy and sweet.' She paused, then gave me a look. 'And they want you there. And if you happen to have any garlands and lights left from the big fancy house, it would be wonderful if you could sneak them in before Hogmanay."

'I'd be honoured,' I said.

'Good. And Amanda's invited too.'

I rubbed the back of my neck, then picked up the needle and resumed stitching.

'She'll have left by then.'

'So I heard. But I'm sure you can convince her to stay a few more days.'

'It won't be on her schedule.'

'Then give her something worth staying for. Folks do crazy things for love.'

'It's not love.'

Jean cracked a cheeky smile.

'They do even crazier things for lust.'

sixteen

> OTTERLEIGH BAY VILLAGE NEWS
> Wrapping has them all fingers and thumbs

AMANDA

By the time the house was quiet with everyone tucked away in their rooms, I was exhausted. And salty. Henry had gotten me all wound up in the morning, and then he'd buggered off all evening. When the clock ticked past midnight, I was still surrounded by patterned wrapping paper, scissors, and tape stuck in small strips all around the tabletop. I winced at another papercut as I wrapped one of the final gifts.

Every gift needed to look perfect for my clients. And I'd already prebought and wrapped the lists of small but expensive presents that could easily be packed in suitcases, but they had all come home from the village market with armfuls of hand-selected gifts.

Which would have been sweet had they also hand-wrapped them. Instead, I'd been stuck in the smaller dining room all evening, wrapping while they had a Scottish folk singer in to entertain them.

My eyes stung from the smoke from the log fire, and I was likely tired too. Or annoyance. Had Henry gone to bed? Leaving me stewing for the night. Perhaps our little tete-a-tete in the orangery had affected him far less than it had me.

'Get a grip,' I scolded myself, wrangling double-sided tape that refused to detach from its roll. I was acting like I should be writing Henry and Amanda in arrowed hearts on the front of a jotter rather than a grown adult.

My elbow caught a gift box, knocking it off the counter and sending it skidding across the floor.

'Oh, fuck off.' I told the box.

I didn't hear Henry come back, not until a low voice broke the quiet, sending me jumping half out of my skin.

'Burning the midnight oil, Amanda?'

My breath caught as Henry leaned against the doorframe, crossing his arms and letting those blue eyes drag slowly over my frame. Snow dusted his shoulders, clinging to his sweater, and the wind had mussed his hair into even wilder curls. He took one look at the chaos surrounding me, then at me - tape stuck to my sweater dress, ribbons tangled around me and to the stack of gifts in the corner.

'Needed something to fill my night.' My voice was more petulant than I'd intended.

'Did you have something more riveting in mind?' Henry crossed the room.

'Wouldn't you like to know?'

Henry closed the space between us, penning me against the table. I swallowed as I looked up at him.

'I imagine it's much like the thoughts that have been plaguing me all day. About me, between your thighs, making you whimper until you scream. Yes?'

My thighs clenched as I nodded. Then I stood on my tiptoes and grasped the back of his neck, pulling him into a kiss that burned with hunger. I couldn't help it. I couldn't wait one more god damned second to touch him.

Henry let out a dark growl, scooping my hips against him and deepening the kiss, those full lips of his driving me crazy. I don't know who taught him to kiss so fucking well, but I needed to send them a bloody gift basket.

'Are on the table,' he demanded when our lips broke, his hands gathering me and lifting me onto the edge of the wooden tabletop.

'I can't, it's covered in—'

Wrapping paper crinkled beneath me when he pulled me roughly against him, his hand supporting my spine as he rocked himself against me.

'Henry,' I moaned, pleasure rocking me. Confirmation I wasn't the only horny one, at least.

'Be a good girl and lie down.'

'Here?'

'If you want to come, Princess, lie down.'

I did. I really, *really* did.

Ribbons shifted, and paper crackled, tape stuck to my tights, and I glanced at the door, which still stood open. Henry followed my look and stormed over to it, closing it and locking it with the large, old key which sat permanently in the lock.

When he made his way back to me, his palm over my lips as he nudged my thighs wide, taking place between them. Lying back and looking up at him, with him *there*, had me trembling.

'You're so wound up, look at you, so needy.'

A helpless breath escaped me. 'Henry... please?'

His nostrils flared as my plea hit him, the word stroking something inside him that made me squirm. Those thick hands grazed over my spread thighs, massaging me higher and higher, pressing the hem of my dress nearly to my hips.

My pulse danced, and I clutched at a ribbon to my left,

Henry noticed.

He picked up one strand and ran it through his fingers, the red satin catching the light.

The ribbon cinched tightly against my skin as he wrapped it around my wrists, a physical reminder that Henry was taking control.

Something I didn't find nearly as troubling as I'd imagined. I relaxed into my silken bonds as he pressed my hands up above my head and held them there, his body flush with mine. His hard cock ground against my tights, sending threads of pleasure darting up my spine.

'God, you're so fucking perfect,' he breathed, his lips brushing my throat.

His mouth found the sensitive spot just below my jaw, his lips so soft. I arched against him, craving more pressure from his hardness.

My eyes fluttered shut.

'You hold so much together every day, let me be the place you come apart.'

Grabbing a pair of scissors, he cut the crotch of my tights, before ripping them apart, exposing my skin and the scrap of lace before. I let out a yelp, but soon forgave the destruction when his hand slid down past my panties, those thick fingers finding my heat and circling it. I quaked on the table, but had no give, sandwiched between the wood and his solid body. Not that there was anywhere else I wanted to be.

I shifted, against his hand, my breath catching as he sank two fingers inside me, his teeth nipping at my throat. The sharp nip made me tense around his fingers, and the heady mix of pleasure and pain sent any remaining thoughts scattering. Henry's low sound of approval hummed against my throat.

'There it is,' he whispered. 'You don't have to pretend with me, Amanda. I see you, baby.'

'Henry...' I whimpered as he curled his fingers, my back arching off the table.

'Not yet,' he demanded, his mouth soothing the place where he'd bitten. 'I want you to ask.'

My cheeks burned.

'I can't.'

'Oh, but you can. And you'll come all the harder for submitting. But first, I want to see you moan.'

Then his fingers moved back up to my clit, where he redoubled his efforts. Tension coiled low in my stomach until he sank his teeth into my throat again. I bit down to catch a cry, my nerves feeling ready to snap as he toyed with me.

'Oh, Amanda. Look how beautifully you react. And these marks. My marks. They suit you so well.'

'More,' I begged, my world narrowing to his sharp teeth, sweet tongue and taunting fingers. I didn't care who heard or who knew; I'd have done anything Henry demanded of me in that moment.

I trembled beneath his touch, his fingers alternating between deep thrusts inside me and tender circling of my clit. When he added a third finger, stretching me deliciously, I nearly came on the spot. But he held me there, right on the edge as I whimpered and moaned.

'Please, Henry. Please let me come.'

'What was that?' he teased, lips brushing my collarbone. 'I didn't quite hear you.'

'Please, ' I whispered through stutttering breaths. 'I need—'

Henry didn't hold back. He slid his thumb over my clit while his other fingers fucked me mercilessly.

'That's it, Princess, give in for me.'

And when he sank his teeth into my throat once

more, I did. The ribbons tightened around my wrists as fireworks exploded behind my eyes, pain and pleasure twisting up inside me until it swallowed me up completely. When my moans increased, he moved to my mouth, kissing me with fervour as he swallowed my noise. And for a few blissful moments, nothing else in the world mattered but the exquisite sensations Henry wrought within me.

It wasn't until I finally dropped back against the counter, all unsteady breath and jellied limbs, that Henry cupped my face, his eyes dark but soft.

'Look at you,' he whispered. 'So perfect like this.'

I blinked up at him, messy and flushed.

He lifted his soaked fingers, watching the way they glistened in the firelight. With a smile, he touched them to my lips, his eyes expectant.

My stomach flipped, and I considered refusing, the expectation making my need for control rear up. Yet, a dirty little part of me wanted to please him like that. To have him know the dark little thoughts that had plagued me half of my life.

And though I should have refused, I didn't.

I opened my mouth and let him drag the wet pad of his finger over my tongue.

His breath caught, his lip catching his lower lip.

'You're going to ruin me,' he murmured.

When he removed his fingers, after I'd slowly tongue-bathed them, I closed my eyes and relaxed back against the mess. 'I'm very much hoping you'll ruin me, Henry.'

seventeen

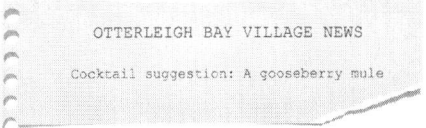

AMANDA

I MIGHT WELL HAVE HAD THE BEST SLEEP I'D HAD IN YEARS after Henry's finger-fest on the dining table. I'd offered to take care of his rather generously erect self when he'd escorted me up the stairs, but he'd declined, telling me it was late and he could wait until we were both a bit brighter-eyed.

We'd lain in bed, me on one side of the wall, and him on the other, texting until I fell asleep with a huge smile on my face and satisfaction still roiling through my body.

The manor felt unusually peaceful the morning

after the Christmas fair. I'd been awake since half past six, unable to rest with so many thoughts racing in my head.

I told myself I was going outside to check the final preparations for Christmas Day.

But it was a lie, of course. I wanted to see him.

I found him beside the stable, breath fogging in the cold air while he brushed hay from Merv's coat. His hair poked out from beneath a woollen hat in ridicuously adorable curls, and his cheeks shone pink from the cold.

Merv saw me first, lifting his head and braying. His ears perked up as he trotted straight over, nudging my side like a giant puppy.

'He likes you,' Henry said with a laugh.

'I hope that's because you've been putting a good word in for me,' I said, petting Merv's forehead as he nudged me harder. 'But it might be because I have a clementine in my pocket.'

'He's selective, so you should be flattered.'

I laughed, and Henry's eyes flicked to me, a delighted grin covering his face.

'What?' I asked.

'I've been waiting to see you smile for real. It's as beautiful as I pictured.'

I tucked a strand of hair behind my ear and flushed.

Henry held out a soft-bristled brush. 'Want to help?'

'He doesn't kick, does he?'

'Not if you're nice to him. I can't guarantee he won't pinch your orange, though.'

Merv nudged my pockets the moment I stepped into the stable. I handed the orange to Henry, who swapped it for a soft-bristled brush.

Our shoulders brushed against each other now and then as we worked, him feeding the donkey and fussing over him, me brushing his soft coat. It was quiet. The kind of quiet that felt comfortable rather than awkward. I ran the brush down Merv's side, watching dust and stray hay fall away.

'You're good with him,' Henry said, his hand grazing mine as I brushed.

'Animals are easy,' I murmured. 'I'm used to trying to corral humans.'

'Good point.'

'I don't actually know much about you, I don't even know how old you are.' It's probably something I should have asked before having him pin me to a table and forget my name.

'Twenty-five.'

I blinked.

'Oh God. I'm nearly thirty.'

'And?' he said, his eyebrows lifted in amusement.

'Am I a cougar? Guys don't usually like older women.'

'Amanda, I lost myself the moment you walked into the manor, looking ready to claw someone's eyes out.'

I winced. 'I was stressed!'

'I *love* your fire, but I love it even more because it makes the moments you let me lead all the more delicious.'

I inhaled sharply, focusing on the brush as warmth diffused through me. 'So you don't expect me to be all docile and sweet out of bed?'

He raised an eyebrow.

'I don't believe we've made it to a bed *yet*.'

My face burned.

He tilted my chin up with one finger.

'No,' he said. 'I don't expect docile. Or sweet. Or tame.'

His voice dropped all growly again, and I clenched my thighs with the memory of the previous night's activities.

'Where's the fun in taming you if you aren't feisty?'

'You're ridiculous,' I said with a roll of my eyes.

'And you *like* it.'

I didn't answer because I couldn't deny it. Despite my initial annoyance at his over-the-top cheeriness, being wrapped in it was like being wrapped in a squishy duvet.

When we finished, Henry dusted his hands off and gave Merv a pat before turning to me again.

'So what's on the cards for the day?'

'Appeasing the clients, making sure everything is set for both Christmas Eve and the big day. Just the usual.'

We stepped out of the stable into a drifting snowfall, the flakes fat and light, dancing down around us.

'I guess the wealthy really can get everything they ask for,' I said, knowing that they'd be thrilled with the change in weather.

Henry's fingers found mine, their roughness reassuring as he slid them into my hand.

'And sometimes, even the gardener does,' he murmured under his breath.

I went back to work with a pep in my step.

eighteen

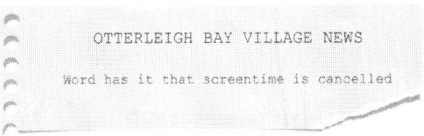

OTTERLEIGH BAY VILLAGE NEWS
Word has it that screentime is cancelled

HENRY

By the time the Petersens finally retreated to their wing of the house full of copious rich foods, brandy cream, and countless glasses of red wine that cost more than I made in a week, I felt like I'd been dunked in a cold bucket of water and shoved through a mangle.

Christmas Eve had drawn to a close, complete with a dramatised retelling of The Night Before Christmas from a local am-dram group, much to the delight of our guests.

I traipsed upstairs twenty minutes past midnight.

My feet hurt.

My back hurt.

And I hadn't managed to steal a kiss from Amanda since lunchtime. I knocked gently on her door as I passed, but there wasn't an answer.

Shutting my door behind me, I pulled out my phone only to see a string of messages from my mother. Seeing that it had officially tipped from Christmas Eve into Christmas Day, she'd demand a call no matter how late.

I hadn't talked to my family in a few days, so I stepped out onto the little balcony off my room to FaceTime them. The signal was always ropey in the oldest wing of the house, where my room was located. I shuddered as cold wrapped around me; it would need to be a quick call.

Mum answered first, all pink cheeks and tinsel crown.

Dad shouted hello from somewhere in the background.

One of my sisters, who was the only one spending both Christmas and betwixtmas with my parents, waved something sparkly that looked a lot like Gus Gus, our old sausage dog.

'You look exhausted,' Mum pointed out.

'Well, a merry Christmas to you too.'

She tutted. 'You need a proper rest. You should come home more often. We miss you.'

'I know, I'll be home in a few days. Just—'

After a few minutes of chatting about the clients and Mum and Dad's visits with the elder relatives, the picture froze, then pixelated. Cut and reconnected. Cut again.

'—Henry? Can you hear us? What's going on?' Mum, Dad and my sister, Grace, filled the screen.

'Signal's rubbish,' I said. 'Hang on, I'll come back inside nd see if it pops in.'

I stepped into the room, half-chatting and half-yelling and set the phone on the desk while rummaging for my charger.

A soft knock sounded at my door, and before I could turn, I heard Amanda's voice.

'Henry?'

I spun around. And everything in me stilled.

There she was.

Standing in my doorway in nothing but underwear and bows. Silken ribbons wrapped around her waist and thighs, one even fastened around her throat.

She looked incredible. A seductive Christmas present all ready to unwrap.

She stepped inside, and I steadied myself against

the wall, my ability to think having fled my addled little brain.

'Merry Christmas,' she said, looking both coy and like a temptress all in one.

Behind me, my mother's voice rang out.

'HENRY? IS THAT A WOMAN? WHAT'S HAPPENING?'

Amanda jolted like she'd been tasered, wrapping her hands around herself before tucking into my ensuite.

I lunged for the phone and tripped on the corner of the duvet, which sent me sprawling over the desk chair.

Amanda poked her head out of the bathroom as I went arse-over-tit.

Mum shouted, 'Henry!'

Dad asked, 'Is he dead?'

The dog barked with wild excitement, and my sister laughed her arse off. I reached up and grabbed the phone, hitting the red symbol.

Silence.

Mortifying silence.

Amanda emerged from the bathroom, her face nearly as red as the ribbons she wore. Her eyes were saucer-wide.

'Henry, I'm so sorry. I didn't want to hang out in

the corridor in case anyone saw me. I shouldn't have let myself in. This was a stupid idea.'

'No. Don't say that.' It took a moment for me to pull myself back to my feet, double-checking the call had ended before shoving it in a drawer.

'I don't know what came over me. I look ridiculous. God, your family saw me like this.'

'They didn't see anything, I'm pretty sure they were facing the bed. They will have just heard your voice. And seen my panic.'

'I just thought I would try being fun, for a change. Do something a bit silly to thank you for being so sweet. Well, and not so sweet too.'

I made my way to her, gathering her up against me and running my fingers over the silk of the ribbons. 'And I adore it. You look amazing, and I'm very much hoping you might still let me unwrap my gift?'

'You're sure I don't look silly?'

'Amanda.' I tilted her chin and brushed my lips over hers. 'You're not silly. You're the most beautiful thing I have ever seen walk through a doorway.'

'High competition too when you spend every day with a donkey.'

Her joke made me laugh, and reassured me she

would be okay. Then her mouth parted, those eyes flicking up to mine.

'So you like it?' she asked.

'I nearly died from delight.'

'Come here,' I said, sliding my hands around her waist and guiding her toward the bed, stopping just short as she wrapped her arms around my neck, her throat bobbing when I traced the edge of one ribbon with my fingertips.

'Let me look at you, baby.'

Stepping away from me, she gave a slow twirl, those ruby ribbons bobbing with each movement.

God damn.

'You did all this for me?' I don't know which god I'd pleased, but whoever it was, I offered them a thank-you.

A nod. 'To please you.'

To please me. Fuck, that sent shivers down my spine.

'And you will, sweetheart. But first, I want to unwrap you.'

Her breath hitched as I caught her around the waist and lowered her onto the bed. The ribbon around her waist went first. I tugged it off and discarded it, kissing a trail across the skin it had covered.

Amanda moaned breathily when I did the same for the ribbons that circled her thighs, taking my time to kiss and lick every ounce of skin I exposed until she was eventually laid in nothing but her red underwear. The temptation to cut it off gnawed at me, but underwear could be expensive, so I unhooked her bra like a good boy.

'Fuck,' I groaned as I circled her nipples, watching rapt as they peaked under my attention. My tongue followed my fingers. Then my teeth. Amanda's back arched as I took my time with her, working her pretty chest until she writhed beneath me.

'Where are you going?' She demanded as I stood, turning off the lights and grabbing a candle from the dresser. Low melting point, my favourite.

'To get a little something I think you'll enjoy.'

I lit the taper, letting the warm glow spill across her skin. Shadows danced over her skin, and she flinched as the wax dripped onto her stomach.

'It won't burn you. Just a moment of heat, and then the sensation grows. Can you feel it?'

'Yes,' she said, her stomach tightening as another drop landed.

'I love it when you give in.' The wax was as red as her ribbons, leaving a trail of droplets from her hip up to her chest. I grew particularly fond of the slutty little moans she gave when the wax dripped on her nipples.

Her breathing grew more rapid with each passing minute, and when I dripped the wax over her thighs, she trembled.

'Henry,' she whispered, barely a breath, 'please...'

And that was it. The last thread of my restraint snapped like the thinnest twig. Placing the candle on the bedside table, I tore off her panties and shoved them into her mouth, enjoying the way her pupils dilated when I did.

Flipping her over, I positioned her at the edge of the bed.

'Grab your ankles, Princess, and don't let go.'

She lay on her stomach, face tipped to one side, splayed open with her ass in the air. Glistening so sweetly for me.

All for me.

'So very wet,' I said, knelt beside the bed and basking in her obedience.

'Henry, please fuck me,' she begged around the wet material of her underwear.

'No. You can't display all that for me and expect me not to have a taste, Amanda. Such a delicious feast, and I want to taste you so very badly. Want to feel you lose control with nothing but my tongue.'

Her gasp was soft, broken and desperate when I leaned forward and pressed my tongue against her. I couldn't tell which one of us moaned the loudest. She tasted sweet and salty and perfect. Her fingers tightened around her ankles, and she wriggled backwards, demanding more with every inch of her body.

'I want to taste the need you've been hiding from everyone else,' I murmured, my lips brushing over her heat and making her squirm. My teasing only lasted so long before I couldn't hold back any longer. My soft touches turned to hungry lashes of my tongue, alternating between nipping her with my teeth and sucking her into my mouth. A light sheen covered her skin, growing hot beneath my fingers as I pressed my arms between her thighs, spreading her even wider and grabbing her ass with my hands.

The perfect position to hold her steady while I made her fall apart.

'You taste so fucking good, baby,' I said against her swollen flesh, delighting in every dirty little gasp she gave. I felt her orgasm before it hit fully, her cunt pulsing against my mouth.

I redoubled my efforts against her clit, teasing the bundle of nerves until she cried out into the sheets, her body flexing and shaking as I swallowed down every last little ounce of her desire.

When I finally released her and gathered her against me, she looked totally boneless. A satisfied puddle of woman. I fished the panty gag from her mouth and tossed it aside.

She touched my cheek with shaking fingers.

'Henry...'

'I've got you,' I whispered, kissing her slowly. 'I'm here.'

She exhaled against my mouth and finally curled up in my lap like I'd hoped she would the day I met her.

And lord help me, it made me fall even harder.

nineteen

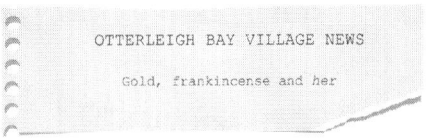

OTTERLEIGH BAY VILLAGE NEWS

Gold, frankincense and *her*

AMANDA

CANDLELIGHT SENT DANCING SHADOWS ACROSS THE ROOM as Henry cradled me in his lap. He seemed perfectly content to relax, but I wasn't finished with him. I'd had two orgasms to his zero, and I was just as desperate to see him come as he'd been to see me. My breathing was still uneven, and my pulse flickered as I whispered against his lips.

'Let me please you too.' Henry pulled back enough for those blue eyes to search my face. For good measure, I dropped my voice lower and added a, *'Sir.'*

The moment he caved was clear as day on his face. 'Whatever the lady wants.'

Lifting me from his lap, he deposited me on the bed and moved across the room to a leather armchair. Sitting, he watched me. While I was completely naked, Henry still remained fully clothed. It only highlighted his stance as the one taking control.

'Come here,' he demanded.

Standing, I took a step forward.

'No, baby.'

He paused.

'Crawl to me.'

For a moment, a flare of defiance seared me. A moment of what the fuck? But seeing him there, leaning back at ease in the armchair, his thick forearm draped over one side, I couldn't help but fold like a well-used deckchair.

My palms met the carpet, and I crawled toward him, my face heating as his teeth caught his lower lip. Never had anyone looked at me with so much unadulterated lust. Despite my current position, his desire made me feel powerful. To have a man so enraptured with me was addictive.

'Beautiful,' Henry crooned as I reached him, kneeling in front of his legs.

His easy praise had me eager to finally get my eyes and other parts on his cock.

Sliding his hand into my hair, he tipped my face to his, lifting me up on my knees until I winced. If I hadn't been wet already, I would have been wet now.

'Tell me what you want, Amanda.'

I swallowed, lips parted, unable to speak.

He reached for his waistband, slowly undoing the button. When he pushed the fabric aside, I caught a wicked glint of metal and my breath caught in my throat. I hadn't in my wildest dreams expected him to be pierced.

'Look at what you do to me?'

Henry pressed me downward until my face was three inches from his cock, close enough to see everything, but far enough that I couldn't touch him.

My cheeks burned.

Using slow, deliberate strokes, he ran his hand over his thickness, his breath thickening with each twist of his wrist. His eyes locked on mine the moment I tore them away from the silver-topped cock.

'You make me ache,' he whispered. 'All day. Every day. I'm supposed to be working, but all I can think about is you on your knees for me.'

A shiver stole over me, large enough that he noticed.

'Do you want this, Amanda?' he asked, his fingers brushing over the tip.

'God, yes,' I whispered. 'Yes.'

The way his jaw tightened had me melting.

'Then come get it.'

Loosening his grip on my hair, he let me shift forward, my hands on his jeans. I kissed the gleaming tip gently before probing at the piercing with my tongue. It was an odd sensation, and I couldn't help what it would feel like *elsewhere*.

The growl he gave made me slide my lips over the swollen tip of his cock, craving more of his pleasure. It was like his every moan fuelled me to take more. Henry let me explore him for a few minutes at my own pace, lathing him with my tongue until he grew veined and fully engorged.

'That's it,' he whispered, using his hold on my hair to guide me. 'Fuck, you're good at this.'

When he pressed my head lower, he let out a shaky exhale that vibrated through every word he spoke next.

'Christ, Amanda...'

Henry's control waned. His hips rocked, slow at first, then with a punishing rhythm that stole my breath. He held me tight, saliva coating us both as he grazed the entrance to my throat.

And greedily, I wanted to take all of him.

'Every time you comply like this, it ruins me a little more.'

My whole body heated at the deep growl in his words, then his tone darkened.

'I thought about this,' he said between thrusts into my mouth, his breath ragged, 'every time you snapped at me. Every time that sharp little attitude flared up. I imagined fucking the attitude right out of you.'

I whimpered, the sound muffled against him.

'Of you here, on your knees, taking every inch like a good girl.'

He shuddered.

'I'm obsessed with you. I spend all day imagining what I'll do to you when the house goes quiet. How I'll take you apart. How I'll fill you—'

My breath caught as he thrust sharply, piercing my throat as I gagged.

Henry tensed, hot cum filling my throat until I coughed and sent it spluttering over both of us in a great white stream.

He exhaled, in a long and slow groan, his fingers stroking the back of my neck as I knelt back and looked up at him. Satisfaction coiled in my chest at the way his face grew so utterly serene.

'Come here,' he said. 'Let me hold you.'

'You're covered in cum.'

'So are you,' he pointed out.

'Good point.'

I curled into his lap and smiled. He pressed his nose to my hair, breathing me in.

'Well, who knew you were hiding all that heat in that sharp little mouth of yours.'

'Wait until you discover what other pleasures I'm hiding.'

'Behave, you. I'm too tired for you to be getting me all horny again.'

I laughed. 'Aren't you the younger man? Shouldn't you be halfway through round two already?'

'Not when you sucked my soul out of my god damned cock.'

'I have a gift for you,' I said. 'Mind if I go shower in my room and bring it through?'

'I don't need a gift, you're gift enough, but go for it. I'll come through in twenty?'

By the time we'd both showered and sat on my bed in the fluffy white Bayview Manor dressing gowns, tiredness nipped at my eyes.

I grabbed the little wrapped bundle from my

dressing table and passed it to Henry, nerves bubbling in my stomach. Would he like it? Or was it stupid?

It took him about three seconds to unwrap the glass donkey ornament, its slightly crooked ears catching the glow of the lamp.

Henry stared at it for a long moment, his fingertip drifting over the wonky glass nose.

'You got this for me?' he asked.

'I thought it looked like Merv. And you love him'

'It does,' he said, turning it over in his fingers like it was precious. 'And I do.'

'And this is for you.' He passed over a lumpy, tissue-wrapped bundle. I took it and fondled its squishy form. My curiosity flared up. He tucked a strand of hair behind my ear, his expression going shy in a way that didn't match the man who'd just had me on my knees.

I tore into the tissue paper and froze.

It was a large, garish Christmas jumper. With a giant golden A on the front. Not exactly something I'd ever wear.

'I, um. Wow.'

Henry laughed. 'I know you said you hated Christmas, but I'm hoping it's a little more bearable this year. And you said that you had never really had the festive pyjamas or Christmas jumpers or any real traditions. I thought this could always remind you of Otterleigh Bay. And me.'

A lump formed in my throat so fast I nearly choked on it.

He wasn't teasing. He'd listened and remembered.

'Well, I suppose things are looking up this year.'

'Put it on,' he said.

The jumper swamped me, but it was warm and soft and a little like Henry.

'Shit, Amanda, you're beautiful.'

'Like this?'

I squeaked when Henry grabbed me and pulled me back on the bed, wrapping himself around me as the jumper rode up just enough that cool air brushed my skin.

'I like seeing you in something of mine.'

'It's hideous.'

'But it's ours now. Something that made me feel welcome, that I hope will make you feel the same.'

I'd never had a Christmas jumper, nor silly traditions. I'd always pretended it didn't matter. That it was stupid.

But lying there, wrapped in something gaudy, felt almost like belonging.

Henry kissed me again, a sweet lingering kiss that

contrasted so thoroughly with the heat from earlier, but felt no less important.

'Merry Christmas,' Henry mumbled into my hair when I turned over.

'Merry Christmas, Henry.'

And outside the window, where I'd forgotten to shut the curtains, I saw snow drifting past the moon. For once, I let myself believe in magic.

Even if it was only for a few days.

twenty

> OTTERLEIGH BAY VILLAGE NEWS
> Merry Christmas to all, and to all a sweet night.

HENRY

Christmas Day arrived with the excitement of small children and the tiredness of adults awoken too early. I'd expected the clients to have taken the morning at a much more restrained pace, and I was pleasantly surprised by the sheer chaos that surrounded me.

But the real difference was Amanda. Everything about her had become more relaxed. The easy way she encouraged the children at breakfast, and the quiet confidence with which she corralled everyone through their perfect Christmas Day. It was like her sharp edges had rounded off just a touch. Not enough that she wasn't still the same brisk, efficient woman, but enough that she wasn't terrifying to approach.

Pru leant against the wall beside me and nudged me with an elbow. 'I don't know what you did to her, but whatever it was, keep it up.'

'Who said I did anything?'

She levelled me with a stare. 'The manor walls might be thick, but they're not soundproof.'

Fuck.

'Sorry.'

'It's alright, Henry, we all do it.'

Well, what do you say to that? Pru had to be nearing retirement, so good for her. I had zero interest in imagining her tied up in ribbons and dripped with candle wax.

I turned my thoughts back to Amanda, who I could see in the vast sitting room by one of the trees. She slipped the little Petersen boy a second candy cane before tapping a finger against her lips when he widened his eyes. Then she made her way to the coffee machine, pouring tall drinks in glasses, and topping them off with a splash of Harris whisky. Nothing but the finest pick me up for the flagging adults.

I made my way down to her and relished in the naughty smile she gave.

'Winter warmer?' she asked. I gladly accepted the fire-laden coffee.

'You're supposed to be the sensible one,' I said as I traced her spine with my spare hand, letting my fingertips follow the bumps upwards before skirting back down. The contact was light, but she leaned into my touch.

'It's Christmas, I'm allowed to be naughty on one day a year.'

'Only one?'

She didn't turn toward me, but I noticed a smile tug the corner of her lips.

'I suppose I could allow for bank holidays, too.'

Those damned lips beckoned, and I couldn't resist stealing the briefest kiss when she looked up at me. A tiny whisper of a kiss, just enough to tide me over until I could steal her away from everyone.

Later, with the family occupied by presents and charades, we slipped into the kitchen to have a mini-celebration with the rest of the staff, both hired in and the regulars like Pru and I.

An impressive spread covered the kitchen island; the chef had made a bit extra of everything he'd served at the family's meal and laid it out for us. Prawn cocktail, with the fattest, pinkest prawns I'd seen. Crab legs and lobster tail. Then there was the traditional feast, turkey surrounded by pigs in blankets and crispy roast potatoes. Caramelised carrots and the inevitable bowl of Brussels sprouts. Cheeses of just about every variety and enough crackers to rebuild Hadrian's wall. Pru poured mulled wine with very little regard for the fact that we were still at work. The tinny speaker in the corner filled the kitchen with the cheesiest of Christmas tunes.

Lisa from next door slipped in not long after we filled our plates. Her shoulders curled inwards as if trying to make herself smaller than her willowy frame allowed. Her blonde hair was loosely braided on one shoulder, and she quietly stood in one corner, hands tucked into the sleeves of her sweater, as if hoping to observe without being observed.

Amanda drifted to stand beside her, shoulder to shoulder, both of them contemplating a platter of the bacon-wrapped sausages. Lisa relaxed at Amanda's quiet proximity, just enough that her fingers emerged and wrapped around a steaming mug of mulled wine. A small shift, but one that brought warmth to my chest. I liked Lisa, but she was very much wrapped in layers of armour. A bit like Amanda had been. But her armour wasn't spiked, it was camouflage, shrinking herself back from the world to her aunt and her bees.

But Amanda had seen through her armour, and I found myself admiring her for it.

By late afternoon, the living room had erupted into a lively, nd very boozy party. The children were out with Pru, feeding Merv his Christmas dinner and brushing him within an inch of his life. Rita was still gushing over a most ridiculously large pom-pommed hat that hat daughter had bought at the market. It bobbed back and forth as she danced with her daughters-in-law to Wizard.

And in the middle of it all, Amanda laughed as Rita pulled her into their giggling ring and demanded she dance with them.

Staring was bad form, but I couldn't help myself. She was like the sweetest flower, drawing me like a pollinating bee.

By the time the Petersens settled into post-party drowsiness, Amanda and I slipped to one of the snugs and collapsed onto the sofa in front of the fire I'd built. She curled her legs beneath her and rested her head against the back of the couch, letting out a happy sigh.

'I don't remember the last time I was this tired.'

I reached out, pulled her feet into my lap, and rubbed my thumbs into their socked arches.

'Oh,' she groaned, her head tipping back and her

eyes closing as she relaxed, her limbs turning as limp as overcooked pasta.

She glanced over at me, her expression soft and uncertain in the firelight. 'Every way you touch me feels so good.'

'Does that scare you?'

'A little.'

The honesty of it surprised me.

We talked for a while, about our families and Christmasses past. The good and the bad. I told her about how my dad refused to let anyone win a board game, and my mum burnt the Yorkshire puddings every year like clockwork. She told me about the noise and the fighting, and how she and her sister had hidden in their rooms when the fighting was at its worst, under their blankets and sharing the chocolate oranges from their stockings.

And somewhere between funny confessions and heavier truths, she pulled her feet from mine and leaned against my chest, staring into the flickering flames. When she finally lifted her eyes again, they were heavy-lidded.

'I'm exhausted, but if you wanted... we could, you know...'

Her cheeks coloured, a soft flush pinking them.

'We could have a quickie.'

The offer was sweet and shy and wildly tempting, and I desperately wanted to say yes. To take her to bed and lose myself in her. But when I looked at her, I saw the sleepiness in her eyes and the vulnerability behind her bravado. The trust that she was beginning to offer me. Capturing her lips, I kissed her with a mixture of heat and restraint.

'No,' I whispered against her lips. 'When I fuck you for the first time... I don't want it quick.'

Her pupils blew wide.

'I want to savour every second of you. Every sound you make. Every look. Every tremble. I want you open and wanting, and with nowhere in the world you'd rather be. So no. No quickie.'

She didn't say anything for a long moment.

Finally, in a barely audible whisper, she said, 'Okay.'

Much later, when the fire had burned to embers and the house was silent, she shifted against my shoulder. 'What are your plans after the Petersens leave?'

'I'll go home,' I said.

She nodded. 'Me, too.'

'Will you go see your family?'

'It's nothing but fighting. Every year. It's easier not to.'

I swept my fingers along her jaw, guiding her face back to mine.

'Come spend betwixtmas with my family and me.'

'Henry, not only do I not know them. But they won't want the stranger they may or may not have seen in her underpants crashing their party.'

'You haven't met them,' I said with a slow smile. 'They'd absolutely love a stranger to moon over. Mum will have you eating burnt Yorkshire puddings before you can say Merry Christmas.'

She smiled. Not a yes, but not a no either.

'Just think about it, you don't have to decide now.' I gave her another slow kiss, relishing in the warmth of her lips.

We stayed like that until the fire all but ran its course, cuddled up on the couch, with her eyes drooping. Her breath settled into a sleepy rhythm against my chest. I should have carried her upstairs, but I relished her body pressing against me. I traced my fingers through her dark hair, twisting the strands around my fingers, and for the first time in a long time, I let myself imagine a future I hadn't dared want before.

A future with Amanda.

A future where she didn't leave.

twenty-one

> OTTERLEIGH BAY VILLAGE NEWS
>
> BREAKING NEWS: The clipboarded dragon isn't afraid of a little snow

AMANDA

For the first time in as long as I could remember, I woke up on Boxing Day without wanting to hide under my duvet all day to avoid the post-Christmas fallout. No hunched shoulders or clenched jaw. No having my mother phone to rant about how we'd spent thirty-seven more minutes with Dad than her.

Bliss.

Instead, opened the curtains with a smile, only to be met by a blanket of white as far as the eye could see. Snow. Damn it, Henry had mentioned snow, but I hadn't been prepared for the thick, fluffy inches that had appeared. Not that it wasn't pretty, it was, but with snow came logistical issues.

Henry was already gone from my bed, having headed down to see Merv and shovel the paths and put down grit. A broken leg would be the last thing we needed.

The house was surprisingly quiet when I made it downstairs. Until I neared the front door. Shrieks and squeals filtered through the solid wood, and I sighed. I hadn't intended to go outside, but I had to check in on my clients, who I'd expected to still be bedded at the early hour. I pulled on a pair of boots and my thickest coat, and I reached into my pockets for my ugly gloves. Thick and cosy, but utterly horrendous.

'Amanda!' Henry shouted as I stepped onto the stairs outside. Cheerful and suspicious.

Before I could answer, something thudded against my thigh.

'Ouch,' I said.

A sea of giggles met me, and a curly blond mop appeared from behind a parked jeep. Then half a dozen smaller heads.

Henry had the audacity to grin.

'Come play!' His hands cupped around his mouth. 'We're having a snowball fight.'

'No thank you,' I yelled back.

The oldest boy immediately lobbed another snowball at me. 'Are ya chicken, Amanda?'

'I'm not chicken.'

The air was crisp and frozen, the snow sparkling like someone had dumped white glitter over the world. Merv pranced about in a winter coat, kicking up the snow much to the children's delight.

Henry stood there with an infuriatingly smug look, and his army of Aussies. I was doomed.

'I think she's chicken, alright,' he said to a chorus of laughter.

'If you hit me with anything—'

WHUMP.

A snowball collided with my shoulder. Henry bent down and gathered another.

'You absolute tw... um... rotter!' I shouted, taking the stairs and bending down to scoop up a handful of soft snow.

'She's joining!' yelled one of the children.

'No, I'm—'

WHUMP.

Another hit my back. I twisted to see a child making a run for it.

'Right,' I declared, balling snow between my hands. 'You want war? You get war.'

Five minutes later, I was in battle. Shrieking and

laughing, slipping and pelting snow at anyone who moved. The kids took sides, switching allegiances to whoever they decided was in the lead at any one time. Merv tried to eat snowballs while children darted around, trying to be stealthy, but mostly failing. Snow clung to our clothes in white clumps, and everyone's noses soon turned the brightest pink.

Henry caught me around the waist when I tried to dodge him and spun me, making me a still target for a volley or snowballs from the children. We teemed up and pelted them back until we grew both frozen and tired. At that point, I turned on Henry and delivered him a glancing snowball to the chest. With all the drama of a Regency gentleman losing a duel, he grasped his chest and tumbled over in the snow.

'Cruel woman!' he whimpered, rolling in the snow as he pretended to be mortally wounded.

'Grow up, ' I said, throwing another snowball right at his head.

He waited until I came close, before darting a hand out and pulling me down into the snow beside him. I went down in a tangle of arms and snow, laughing as he rolled us over. He hovered over me for a moment, his breath fogging the air and his eyes giving far too much warmth to be socially acceptable.

'Having fun?'

'Shut up,' I said, but I couldn't wipe the stupid smile off my face.

Finally, frozen and soaked, we headed inside. Hot chocolate appeared from the kitchen, loaded with marshmallows, cream and a knowing look from Pru. The kids cuddled under tartan blankets, while I went to stand as close to the fire as possible. Turning like a rotisserie chicken to warm both sides.

Rita appeared right as the kids were finishing their drinks, and our toes and noses began to thaw.

'You look happy today,' she said.

'I think I might be.'

She glanced toward Henry, who helped a young child untangle himself from three colourful scarves.

'He reminds me a bit of my husband when he was young. Steady. Kind. Mischief behind those blue eyes.' Her eyes crinkled. 'Don't let that one go.'

I almost spilt my hot chocolate.

'Oh, we're not—'

'That's what people always say when they don't want to admit a thing is already happening.'

Henry looked over at me across the room, all rolled up sleeves and muscled thighs. For once, I realised that maybe I wasn't trying to survive Christmas, but actually enjoying it.

twenty-two

> OTTERLEIGH BAY VILLAGE NEWS
> And then there were two

HENRY

THE PETERSENS LEFT JUST AFTER BREAKFAST ON THE twenty-seventh, which was a mercy for everyone's sanity. They operated on a strange kind of frantic joy that left the rest of us hollowed out like pumpkins.

They hugged both Amanda and me. The children with slightly sticky hands from the candy canes we'd loaded them up with, the adults swearing they'd be back next year if the Leadbetters would have them. Rita had teary eyes, thanking us for giving her family a taste of the Christmasses she'd remembered, and not another stuffy holiday without soul.

Amanda actually looked touched, her strict composure crumbling further.

It hit me a lot harder than I thought it would, seeing her knocking down those walls she'd surrounded herself in.

As the elaborate gates shut behind their cars, it felt like the whole estate breathed a sigh of relief. Amanda rubbed her forehead before leaning against me.

'I could sleep for a week.'

'You gave them an experience they'll never forget,' I said, wrapping my arm around her shoulder and squeezing her. 'You didn't snap once today.'

'I snapped, multiple times. I'm just getting better at not doing so externally.'

She was frayed around the edges, from stress and pressure, but also from the fact that we still hadn't slept together. Delaying the moment only made her crave it all the more, and I relished in the long looks and tremble of her fingers as she touched me.

Which made what I did next all the more evil.

I ran my nose along her jaw, murmuring against her throat.

'If you're good at my parents' house, we'll come back afterwards, and I'll fuck the holiday spirit right into you.'

Her lips parted into a tiny, startled gasp that went straight to my spine as I sank my teeth into tender flesh.

'Henry...' she whimpered, already on the edge.

I stepped back, delighted. 'Something to look forward to.'

The house needed righting, and the decorators had arrived to undecorate with boxes, ladders, and dubious expressions when they saw the additional decorations we'd added to the tree.

Pru moved through the manor armed with an industrial bin bag and a no-nonsense attitude, while Amanda and I plunged headfirst into mayhem.

Cheesy nineties hits played through hidden speakers, the manor bordering on a party as we worked. When the decorations were removed, anything living was put aside to decorate the secret wedding.

'You're very sparkly,' I said when we let the cleaners in, stopping to pick some tinsel from Amanda's hair.

'An unfortunate side effect of the job.'

'You say that, but you looked thrilled this morning when you were humming along to the music.'

'I did no such thing.'

'You did, I was watching *very* closely.'

She threw a cloth at my head.

By the time the house was restored to some semblance of the pristine home he and the Leadbetters had maintained, Pru and the chef headed off for a well-earned break with their own families. Pru left with a warning to behave ourselves and a wink.

Amanda and I stood alone in the expansive kitchen, leaning against the counters, like two people who had run a marathon with no training.

'Hungry?' I asked.

'Is there anything left?'

I pulled open the fridge and smiled. There sat the catering tray of leftover untouched food, but for the one scoop Pru had helped herself to before she left.

'Please tell me we're eating that straight from the tray.'

I fetched two spoons. 'Naturally.'

We took our positions on the floor, backs against the cabinets and the tin straddling our laps in a reminder of the night we first kissed. A few short days before, but that felt like an eternity ago at the same time. Amanda scooped a creamy, coffee-laden bite, and groaned softly. I tried not to let the way the sound affected me show.

'So, fill me in on this betwixtmas situation.'

I helped myself to a spoonful of heaven while admiring her. How pretty she looked in the half-light, those inky dark eyes lined with smudged kohl.

'My family are fiercely competitive,' I said. 'Board games. Quiz nights. Anything involving dice. Anything involving cards. Anything that can be scored and thus won'.

'I like them already.'

'They cheat. They'll play emotionally if it makes you stumble. They will absolutely weaponise any weaknesses you show.'

'Should I be worried?'

'Yes. Don't let them win. Ever.'

She raised a brow. 'Is that why you're bringing me? To shore up your terrible gamesmanship?

'Of course. Not at all because you've come in and bewitched me like a devilish Scottish sprite.'

She blushed and sighed, *'Henry,'* her voice low.

Then she smiled. It was the smile that made me think that maybe, just maybe, she was going to say yes.

To Betwixtmas.

Perhaps, to something more than a holiday fling.

We ate the tiramisu in easy silence, pressed against each other while the whole world shrank to the two of us. And one thing I knew for sure was that if she came with me, there would be no coming back from it for either of us.

    I wasn't sure there was already.

twenty-three

> OTTERLEIGH BAY VILLAGE NEWS
>
> Notice: Scruff's favourite stick is missing.
> If you've borrored it please return to the beach asap

AMANDA

As we drove into the second hour of our journey, the snow settled more heavily around us. Hillsides and hedgerows were coated white until the world looked like it had been sifted with icing sugar.

Nerves rippled through me as I shifted in my seat. I was on my way to meet Henry's family. The people who had made the man who smiled at me like I was precious. The man who whispered filthy things into my ears and tied me up with ribbons. How do you face that when you aren't even officially a couple? Just a... well, whatever we were. A holiday fling? A few days of recklessness. I didn't know what we were, but I knew it wasn't going to be easy to quantify to all the people who loved Henry.

I twiddled my fingers in my lap, my thumbs worrying at the soft wool of the sparkly Christmas jumper Henry had gifted me. Trying not to think about how I had agreed to do this. To walk into a stranger's family Christmas as though I was some social butterfly and not a dusty Christmas moth. I hoped the sparkly jumper would trick them all into thinking I was a butterfly too. 'You're very quiet.'

'I'm thinking.' My voice lacked the levity I'd hoped for.

'Dangerous,' he teased, but it was threaded with the kind of affection that made my chest ache.

I watched the way fat snowflakes danced lazily past the windscreen.

'I don't know how to do the whole happy family thing. The chaos, the hugging, the million conversations at once. I never know if I'm supposed to say something or stay quiet. I'm not very good at it.'

He didn't brush off my fears. He just reached out and placed one large hand over my thigh, squeezing gently.

'You don't have to be good at it. You just have to be you, and they'll love you.'

I studied his profile, the masculine line of his jaw and the sincerity in those blue eyes.

'How can you possibly know that?'

He didn't hesitate. 'Because it's impossible not to.'

Those words slipped into my chest, making my heart flutter. I was sure he hadn't meant it like *that*, but it didn't stop my stupid pulse from marching like a school band. Turning my attention back to the zipping countryside beyond the window, I hid the apprehension from him, but from the way his thumb drew circles against my thigh, I figured he might have sussed me.

Eventually, his family home came into view. A large stone cottage draped in snow, smoke curling from the chimney and fairy lights glowing from the eaves. It looked like something straight out of an illustrated storybook. Some enchanted cottage where fae lingered in the garden, kelpies ran through the evening mist.

The kind of house kids dreamt about while stuck in their box room, avoiding the arguments.

Snow crunched beneath our feet as we got out of the 4x4, the front door bursting open, and who could only be Henry's mum, spreading her arms. She had the same golden curls and pink cheeks, and the same sunshine smile. Her robin-coated apron flapped in the wind, and she looked like she'd been standing at the door for hours, waiting for her boy to arrive. She hurried toward us across the snowy path with snow getting in her slippers, her face beaming.

'Henry! You made it. Your dad was saying that the roads are treacherous, but I told him you've made it home. You always do.' She pressed her hands to his cheeks and pulled him down to her height to plant a kiss on his forehead. 'You're freezing, get inside. And this must be Amanda?'

She didn't wait for an answer, enveloping me in a hug so warm and soft that I nearly forgot she was a stranger. The kind of hug I imagined Mrs Claus herself would give. The kind of hug I had never once been on the receiving end of in real life from my own mother. She hugged me, but while always leaning away a little, keeping some space between us. And never more than three seconds. I'd counted, as a child. Sometimes I still did.

Mrs James' hug lasted for a full seven seconds. No wonder Henry was so bloody jolly.

'Lovely to meet you, sweetheart,' she said into my hair. 'You can call me Betty. Come on, the fire's on. Let's get you two warmed through.'

I followed her inside, immediately hit by a wave of noise that nearly knocked me backwards. The house was *alive*. Like that scene in Home Alone when all the cousins were there and it was sheer pandemonium. Was I Kevin? I hoped not. Children ran in erratic loops between rooms, a teenager chased after them, wielding a broom as a sword, while two dogs fought over a squeaky turkey toy, and laughter bubbled from every direction. Someone shouted about a burnt cake, and Betty went off toward the kitchen. A wizened old lady argued with an old man about thermostat settings while one of Henry's sisters greeted him with a shout that sounded like both affection and threat.

I stood in the doorway like a tourist watching a safari.

And then they spotted me.

'Is this Amanda?'

'Oh, she's lovely, Henry.'

'Do you want tea, dear? Something stronger?'

'We'll need to find another chair.'

'Or put Henry on the kids' table.'

'Mum, *stop fussing*!'

It was too much. Too loud. Too warm. Too everything. I didn't know who to talk to first, them all merging into one voice. I was torn between ducking behind Henry and running back into the snow.

He saw it right away.

Of course.

He always sees me.

He closed the distance between us and put that steadying hand on my lower back. To anyone else, it likely looked casual, but it grounded me amongst the chaos. His breath brushed my ear.

'You're alright,' he whispered. 'You'll soon filter through the loud.'

'Loud?' I whispered back. 'It's practically noise pollution.'

He smiled, his hand staying exactly where it was.

The terror eventually morphed from overwhelming to welcomed. Folded into the family as though I had always belonged there.

The evening fell into a rhythm I had never experienced before, where arguments fell easily into laughter, children climbed onto laps without being shooed off, and grandparents dispensed sweeties with a soft smile. The kitchen table groaned under the weight of leftovers. Betty might have a propensity to burn Yorkshire puddings, but she certainly made up for it in sheer quantity of food.

Henry's father told a story about a turkey disaster that had me choking on my drink. At various intervals, people kept touching my arm affectionately as we spoke, fully invested in what I had to say. Being in the James home was being surrounded by love. Overwhelmed by it.

It shouldn't have felt like home. I'd only known the family for a few hours, but everything in me relaxed. I found myself laughing with his sisters and playing cards with his grandmother, who definitely cheated.

Henry was never more than a few feet away from me. Ready to swoop in whenever I looked remotely uncomfortable. He wove in and out of the room, chatting to everyone, both young and old, giving piggybacks and dispensing pretty packages he'd brought. Every now and then, he'd sidle up beside me, his fingers finding mine.

Later, in the living room, the family decided to play charades with the most competitive teams I'd ever seen. A brutal, cutthroat game that slightly terrified me. Betty announced she would tolerate no cheating this year, which immediately set off arguments from people who were clearly planning to cheat or accused others of historical cheating. Apparently, the great charades debacle of 2017 still hadn't been settled. Henry pulled me onto his lap in an armchair.

'Watch or play?' he asked.

'Watch. I don't think I'm quite ready for active participation.'

'A good choice,' he whispered. 'They become feral during games.'

He wasn't exaggerating.

I had never in my life seen such competitive energy. There was shouting. Accusations. Victory dances and more than one set of flipping birds. One of his sisters performed a charade so violently when her team couldn't figure it out that she sent a slipper flying into the Christmas tree. A child clambered onto Henry's lap next to me, midway through a round, yawning sleepily and placing her sweet little hand in mine.

And through it all, Henry kept me giggling. Kept me involved. Certainly kept my fizz topped up.

I loved how protective he was, without being domineering. Outside of the bedroom at least.

'Having fun?' he whispered when the child fell asleep against my arm, her. Pink little cheek hot against me. The sweet curve puffing out with each sleepy breath.

'I am. Thank you for inviting me.'

'They're a lot,' he said, eyes gleaming, 'But they already adore you.'

'They *barely* know me.'

'Time doesn't matter when people find what they want; they see what I see.'

I swallowed hard. 'And what's that?'

His eye contact never wavered.

'Someone worth bringing home.'

And sitting in a room full of loud, loving family, Henry wrapped his arm around me, holding me close as we enjoyed the chaos together. I realised I might be falling so fast I couldn't stop things from snowballing.

twenty-four

> OTTERLEIGH BAY VILLAGE NEWS
>
> Lisa has requested any left over parsnips be donated to Merv.
> But stay downwind of Bayview.

HENRY

The house was still half asleep when I headed downstairs the next morning. The heating hadn't quite kicked in yet, so the kitchen tiles were chilly underfoot. The whole place smelled faintly of last night's dinner and the sourness of wineglasses that hadn't been washed yet.

I thought I'd be the first one up, but I found Mum already standing at the sink. She swayed along to the radio, her sleeves rolled up, and her hands sank into the suds. Dishes stacked precariously on the counters, bowls, plates, glasses, even bits of confetti and discarded paper crowns. I spied a stray piece of glittered wrapping paper and grinned. Dad swept up wrapping paper with intense precision, ready to recycle it as soon as it hit the floor; he'd be most irritated to see a piece had escaped.

'Morning,' I said, kissing Mum on the cheek and grabbing a tea towel.

The lines around her eyes crinkled. 'Morning, duck. You're up early.'

'Couldn't sleep.'

'Didn't think you would', she laughed, passing me the first wet tray straight from the sink.

I took it, as I swiped the towel over it before we worked through the rest. There was something comforting about it, the clink of the dishes and the quiet routine. It was like being young again, so often had I been the first up with Mum, helping her clean after one of their raucous parties. The two of us side by side, chatting about life, or nothing.

Minutes later, she broke the silence in that way that only mothers can. Sounding casual, but darting through to your innermost worries with precision.

'So, tell me about Amanda.'

'What about her?' I asked, trying for non-commital and failing miserably.

Mum chuckled, far more amused than sympathetic. 'Don't play dumb, Henry. It doesn't suit you. I haven't seen you look at someone like that since you were a teen who fell in love with every pretty girl you saw.'

I sighed. 'Mum. I was an idiot at fifteen.'

'Mmm, so spill. Who is she to you? You've never seriously brought a woman home to meet us.'

I dried slowly, feeling the question twisting the doubts I already had.

'She's...' I swallowed. 'She's everything. She's strong, and sharp, and more guarded than she wants people to realise. She carries so much on her shoulders she forgets how to set anything down. And she's also sweet, and soft, and so perfect beneath all the armour.'

Mum's smile widened. 'You're smitten'.

I huffed out a laugh. 'Yeah. I think I am.'

'Is she your girlfriend?'

I paused mid-dry of a bowl, because I'd been avoiding that question inside my own head.

'Not in so many words,' I said. 'We haven't put a name on anything. It's very new.'

Mum glanced at me.' And yet you brought her home.'

I shrugged. 'I didn't really think it through. It just felt right. And I wasn't ready to let her leave yet.'

Mum turned the tap off and dried her hands on her apron, leaning back against the counter.

'Henry, you don't bring someone home because they need somewhere to go. You bring someone home because you want them to accept you and where you come from.'

She wasn't wrong. I wanted Amanda to want me. To want all of this.

'I'm sure about her,' I said, the words out of my mouth before I could second-guess them. 'Pretty sure. No. Completely sure, if I'm honest. I don't know how to explain it, Mum. I've never known anyone like her. I feel like I've been waiting for her without knowing I was waiting.'

Mum's face softened, full of love and pride.

'Good,' she said quietly. 'Because she looks at you like she's smitten too.'

I blinked. 'You think?'

'I don't think, Henry,' she said with a little smirk. 'I know. I've been watching her just as much as you've been watching her. Every time you moved into a room, she relaxed. Every time you weren't looking, she watched you rapt until you were back by her side.'

'She might be scared,' Mum added softly. 'I can see that too. But she likes you a lot. And she trusts you. That's rare, Henry. Don't take it lightly.'

I swallowed, feeling something fierce and protective rise in me.

'I won't. I'd never hurt her.'

'I know you wouldn't.' Mum leaned over and touched my cheek with her slightly damp hand. 'Just be patient with her. Not everyone is ready to go all in so soon.'

I nodded.

Outside, the snow began again in slow, lazy flakes.

Upstairs, I could hear the soft shuffle of someone moving around the office, coming from the box room. Amanda waking up, maybe trying to figure out how to face the day in a house full of people when she's not slightly sozzled.

And suddenly, I was unshakeably sure about wanting more with her in a way I hadn't been the day before.

twenty-five

> OTTERLEIGH BAY VILLAGE NEWS
>
> Remember to look out your gladrags for the Hogmanay ceilidh. Rumour has it, it's not one to be missed

AMANDA

I WOKE EARLIER THAN I MEANT TO, COCOONED SOMEWHERE between the scratchy warmth of the ancient tartan blanket and the sad, deflating sigh of the blow-up bed beneath me. The office was more of a catch-all storage room with a desk shoved against one wall. Papers rustled faintly where we'd stacked them out of the way, a tangle of extension cords coiling to my left, and the faint hum of the old radiator made the space feel like it was alive.

The house beyond the door was quiet, full of sleeping bodies and muffled sounds. Floorboards creaked, a distant kids' cartoon talked in squeaky, muffled voices. A dog gave a sleepy huff somewhere beyond my door. I lay there for a few minutes fighting the urge to pee, and find Henry. My breath fogged above me, warning me to stay tucked up and cosy.

But my throat was dry, and my bladder cried out for relief. The blow-up mattress gave a resigned wheeze as I fought to stand. The bed shifted every time I moved. I found one of Henry's sweaters and pulled it on over my pyjamas, shivering from the chill.

I padded down the corridor, socked feet cold against the wooden floorboards, careful not to disturb the little pockets of sleeping people scattered throughout the house. Every room was bursting to overflowing with family members, and the air still felt thick with the warmth of yesterday's fun. I wasn't used to this kind of familial closeness, so many people under one roof.

Halfway down the stairs, I slowed. Henry's voice drifted up from the kitchen. A murmur meant for someone other than me.

I should have kept walking to the bathroom or made some noise so they knew I was there. Anything other than listen in. I paused, one hand on the bannister, my breath held just a little too tightly.

And that's when I heard my name.

'...Amanda.'

A wash of heat prickled across my chest.

His mum made a soft, amused noise before speaking more words I couldn't quite make out, and then Henry replied, his voice low and unguarded in a way that made my pulse trip.

'She's everything.'

My hand tightened on the bannister, breath catching in the middle of my throat.

But then he continued talking. Lots I couldn't make out, and then one sentence I could.

'I feel like I've been waiting for her without knowing I was waiting.'

The warmth vanished, as if someone opened a window into a blizzard.

It was supposed to be a fling. Just two people enjoying each other for a few days.

My stomach clenched. The worst part was that he wasn't wrong. Everything had moved so fast. *Ridiculously fast.* Too much like a snow globe romance, trapped together by circumstance. Desire in a pressure cooker. Not something that could be expected to last. He'd soon see the real me. The messy woman with nothing to offer but a good paycheque and a busy job. No big, sweet family to bring him home to, or perfect girlfriend vibes where I'm an excellent cook. My sister largely kept our flat clean, and when I wasn't working I mostly survived on ready meals.

His mum murmured something soothing, but the sound blurred in the buzz of blood rushing in my ears.

I stepped instinctively backwards, trying not to make the stairs creak, and drew back into the corridor as quietly as I could. Each step made the house seem narrower as though the air itself had thickened with Henry's admission. Opening up to his mother made it all far too real than I was ready for. Because I would be going home, and he'd be staying in Otterleigh Bay.

By the time I had reached the office and slipped inside, closing the door quietly behind me, my lungs felt like I'd inhaled a tub of golden syrup.

I collapsed back onto the blow-up bed, the plastic groaning beneath me, its uneven shape tilting and rolling me right onto the wooden floor. It felt right, somehow messy, just like me.

I stared up at the ceiling, trying to pick through my emotions, which felt stuck together like a bag of partially melted boiled sweets. It wasn't anger. Or betrayal. It was a mix of wanting him as badly as he wanted me, but knowing that I wasn't looking to settle down. I'd come to Bayview Manor to escape my sad life, not to add more complications to it. I was torn between following my heart and giving Henry and me a chance, and shutting things off before we both fucked it up and hurt each other. Was it better to risk the pain, or enjoy our fling for what it was?

I pressed a hand to my sternum, trying to slow my erratic breathing.

I'd let myself get carried away with the closeness, the snow, the kisses and one deliciously pierced cock. I'd lost myself in desire, sinking into the heady world of Henry and his sweet demeanour, which masked his pain and pleasure-filled Dom side.

It was fast. Intense. I'd been caught up in his ropes and pulled under with his heady current. And I couldn't even blame him, and he'd done the same.

But the truth was that I'd already begun falling for Henry. And I didn't know what to do with that. He was younger than me, and what if I was mistaking lust for something more?

I curled onto my side, pulling the blanket up to my chin. I just needed a minute to breathe and figure out a way to walk back downstairs and pretend I hadn't overheard him. Pretend that he hadn't just cracked whatever was happening open to the world.

twenty-six

> OTTERLEIGH BAY VILLAGE NEWS
> Signage on the village hall has not been approved by the committee. Jean, what are you up to?

HENRY

The first thing I noticed on the drive back into Otterleigh Bay was how quiet Amanda had become.

Not cold, just distracted, like she was over-analysing everything again. She still smiled when I spoke, still teased me, still nudged my elbow with hers in the car, but something in her had tucked itself away. A little wall.

I didn't push.

I wanted to.

But I held back.

She'd promised to come to the ceilidh-come-secret wedding, largely to check whether I'd be going as a true Scot. Plus, she wanted to see Claire and Owen's secret wedding, having never experienced something quite as wild as that. She wanted to be here.

She wanted *me* here.

But every so often, when she thought I wasn't looking, she stilled, retreating into her thoughts.

Amanda's default setting was not still. She sparkled and bristled and busied. When she was quiet, something was weighing her down.

Still, she came with me without hesitation when Owen asked us to prep the village hall for the "Hogmanay decorations" that were actually the basis for the secret wedding decor.

We spent half the evening up ladders, convincing thousands of fairy lights and metres upon metres of leafy garlands to stay in place. She cracked jokes with Jean and Jim, and put her event organisation to swift practice, making a multitude of suggestions that would make the night even more special for Owen and Claire.

The village hall was unrecognisable by the time we finished. The ceiling looked like a star-studded forest canopy. And Claire and Owen thanked us a million times, telling us we'd both have whisky for a while. Amanda looked slightly green at the thought of all that whisky.

Lanterns lined the windowsills, complete with electric candles, much to Amanda's dismay. Jean had told us that the village committee would have a conniption if there were real frames, and the last thing we needed was Morag brandishing a fire extinguisher at the bride.

By the time we'd finished, the place looked truly magical.

I stepped down from the ladder, dusting my hands, and caught Amanda standing in the centre of the room with her gaze tilted upwards. The soft gold of the lights washed over her face, thousands of catchlights glimmering in her dark eyes. She looked dreamy. And that wasn't a word I would have applied to her last week.

'Ready?' I asked.

She turned, her eyes focusing as if she had been miles away.

Probably thinking.

More likely overthinking.

'Can we test it?' she asked. 'With all the other lights off?'

'Sure.' I crossed to the far wall, where the rank of light switches lives, switching off all the main lights, leaving just the fairy lights and the slowly spinning disco ball, which Amanda had fitted with warm white light rather than silver.

It was like being tossed into another world. For being a village hall, the room had been transformed into a truly enchanting space. Even I was awed.

Golden light rippled overhead; the fairy lights twinkled slowly to create a blanket of magic, while the disco ball threw moving lights around the room. Not a single space lacked dancing gold. Lanterns flickered warm and soft. Garlands covered the sketchily painted white ceiling, dulling its brightness and letting the lights stand out. The dark panelled walls reflected the light back at us until the whole space felt enchanted, like a place made for making promises and stolen kisses.

Amanda took a quiet breath. 'It's perfect.'

I crossed the floor to her, unable to resist the pull. She didn't move as I approached, just watched me with that half-guarded, half-yearning expression that had been haunting me since we got back from my parents.

I held out a hand and waited to see if she'd take it. When she did, I pulled her close to me, gathering her with one hand while I held her other against my chest.

'May I have this dance?' I asked.

Her eyebrows knitted. 'There's no music.'

'I don't need music. Just you.'

I began moving in small steps that carried us in circles. Amanda followed my lead, her cheek brushing against my jaw.

The lights glowed around us. The patter of her heart quickened beneath our hands. Mine too, no doubt.

After a few minutes, I brushed a kiss over her temple.

'You're quiet. Somewhere else, maybe. Are you alright?'

She tipped her head back to look at me. Her eyes sparkled with light, her pupils huge and unreadable. Then she smiled.

She said, 'I'm okay. Really.'

I didn't quite believe her, but I didn't want to press and ruin the moment.

Instead, she slid her hands up my chest until they came to rest on the back of my neck, fingers lacing gently into my hair. The shift in her expression hit square below the belt. Wherever she had been in her head, she came out of it looking ravenous.

'You still haven't rewarded me,' she said, almost innocently.

'For what?' I played dumb, knowing well the games that still lay beneath the surface.

'For being so very jolly at Betwixtmas.' Her lips curved. 'Have you gone off me already? Do I need to find another pierced gardener to make me see stars?'

She was teasing, but jealousy flared hot in my chest anyway. I knew she was joking, but Amanda was *mine*.

Low sound rumbled out of me as I traced her lips with mine. 'Princess... I'm going to make you see more than stars. You're going to soar high enough to fuck amongst them.'

The way she trembled had me hard right there in the village hall.

Then she whispered, her voice a soft, warm, lethal thing:

'Don't worry. I have plans for you tonight.'

Her body tightened in response, exhaling deeply to calm herself. I loved how very eager she was to get back into my bed.

I tipped her chin up with two fingers, letting my gaze linger on her mouth, the mouth that had tortured me every day since we'd met.

'You have plans?' she asked so coyly that it took everything not to pin her to the floor and take her in the middle of the village hall. Not that I think she'd have stopped me. Instead, I nudged a leg between hers and gripped her hips to grind her against me.

'Oh, yes,' I breathed.

Amanda whimpered, arching her hips to gain more friction against my thigh.

'Look how horny you are, pressing that sweet cunt against my thigh in public just to show me how needy you are.'

Her cheeks reddened, but she didn't cease the grinding. Gripping her hips tighter, I moved her harshly, enjoying the way it made her gasp.

'This is what you need, isn't it, Amanda? To get out of your head and let me take care of your wet pussy. Right?'

Her answer was a throaty moan that had me biting my lip. I gripped her chin and tilted her face to mine. 'That's it, Princess, get yourself all good and read for me. Nice and wet so you can take every inch.'

Outside, the wind pressed against the hall walls, and inside, the hall filled with her wanton moans as her hips quickened.

'Look. At. Me,' I growled, needing all of her focus as she fell apart. Those dark eyes fixed on my face as her lips opened in a desperate plea.

'Please, Sir. I need all of you.'

Without another word, I hoisted her over my

shoulder, ignoring the wet patch on my thigh. I hit the lights off and locked the hall, all while she whimpered against my shoulder.

Never had the drive back to Bayview seemed so eternally long.

twenty-seven

> OTTERLEIGH BAY VILLAGE NEWS
>
> When the Manor's a-rockin,
> don't go a-knocking.

AMANDA

When we stepped back into the manor that evening, the quiet hit me first.

It was strange and slightly unnerving to be in such a huge house with so few people. Just the two of us.

Henry shut the door behind us, his key turning in the lock as I hung up my coat and kicked off my boots. He did the same beside me, our moment of heat in the hall lingering between us, unspoken. The moment he turned toward me, it was like someone turned a screw, upping the sexual tension.

He watched me with hunger in his face, the kind that throbbed with unbridled desire. The kind that made my pulse stutter in my throat.

'So,' I said lightly, forcing my voice to behave even while my insides fluttered, 'you mentioned some plans?'

The pink of his tongue darted over his lips as he took a step toward me. My stomach knotted. It was bad enough I'd been left right on the edge of orgasm, but when he looked at me like that, it left me a puddle.

His shoulders rolled subtly back, and his mouth curved into a devastatingly sinful smile.

'Oh, I definitely did,' he murmured, stepping toward me with a slowness that made every inch of my skin tighten in anticipation.

I swallowed, struggling to find breath. 'And what exactly do these plans entail?'

He reached out, fingertips grazing my throat. The touch was feather-light, as though he wanted to make me lean into it on my own. And I did, moaning as he wrapped the sides of my neck tight enough to send pleasure skirting through me.

'I'm going to catch you,' he whispered, the words hot against my cheek. 'And I'm going to fuck you. Wherever that may be.'

An involuntary sound that was halfway between a squeak and a whimper. He was going to chase me. It was risky enough in my client's home, but I knew that Henry knew the house well enough to know if it was safe. My thighs clenched at the wicked way he looked at me.

For one suspended heartbeat, neither of us moved until I leaned forward and kissed him, pouring all my heat into his perfect mouth. Within a few heated strokes of my tongue, his fingers relaxed against my throat, and that's when I took my chance. Shoving him hard, I made a break for it, the flagstones slapping beneath my feet.

I didn't give a sexy run, all dainty and playacting. I *bolted,* full speed down the corridor as adrenaline pulsed through me. Hair flying and heart pumping.

Behind me came the most delicious sound, his surprised laugh turning into a feral growl,

the thud of his feet against the floor. The unmistakable rhythm of a man giving chase with one thing on his mind.

'Amanda!' he called, his voice echoing through the hall. 'Princess, you're wasting your time. I'll have you on the floor in seconds.'

I darted around a corner, nearly wiping out on a rug, just catching myself on the wall before sprinting onward. Lamps cast warm pools of light across the old floorboards. Shadows flickered past me as I ran into the drawing room, skimming around furniture like my life depended on it.

For a few glorious seconds, I actually thought I'd lost him.

Then an arm slid around my waist from behind, tightening until I felt just how excited Henry was against my back.

'Got you,' he breathed, voice dark.

He spun me against the wall and pressed his mouth to mine, all molten heat and unrestrained hunger. I gave in to him, melting beneath his touch. When he slid a hand beneath my dress, I arched off the wall, aching for more.

It was molten — a claiming without pressure, a question and an answer all at once.

I arched into him, fingers curling into the fabric of his shirt, unable to stop the hungry sound that slipped out of me.

But some feral little part of me wanted to provoke him. So I bit down on his lower lip until I tasted metal. Just a slight nip, really, but enough that his hold lapsed.

A beat of silence throbbed between us as he

touched his finger to his lip and viewed the red it left. A sharp inhale. And then a low and *dangerous* laugh.

'Oh, you're going to regret that,' he whispered.

I slid out from under his arm and ran again.

This time, the chase didn't last long. He stormed after me, my socks slipping on the flagstones as I hit the bottom of the main staircase. Halfway up, he grabbed my foot and set me stumbling forward, both of us landing on the stairs, him pinning me.

My half-hearted writhing was no match for his strength.

'You're an animal!' I gasped between hysterical laughter.

He adjusted his grip, hauling my dress high and exposing my ass to the house. Using his thighs to pin my legs together, he landed three heavy spanks to my backside, my breath whooshing out as I moaned.

'That's for biting me.'

I heard a zip behind me, his legs keeping mine pinned tightly together.

'And this,' he said, sliding the metal-coated tip of him against my heat, 'Is for being such a beautiful, wild little thing.'

I quaked against the stairs as he teased me, rubbing his piercing over my clip, then up to my entrance, then maddeningly back downward to my clit again.

'Henry,' I begged, losing any semblance of wanting to run. I needed him like I needed to fucking breathe.

The house felt bigger as we lay on the stairs, every creak and noise amplified. Each of his breaths made me writhe. I tried to move backwards, but he used one hand to pin my chest to the wooden treads while continuing to slide the head of his cock over me until I moaned.

'I've thought about this moment again and again. About how it would feel to have you wet and begging for me.' Henry slid into me in one ragged movement. With the way he had me pinned, the feel of him sliding into the tightness made me cry out. The stretch was delicious, and he held himself there, fully enveloped in me. Both of his hands moved to the small of my back, holding me still.

Too still.

His fingers trembled against my waist.

'Don't fucking move,' he said, his voice thick with need. 'I should have used a condom, and if you move even one inch, I'm pretty sure I'm going to coat your insides.'

Heat hit my cheeks.

'Have I got you so wound up, Sir?' I teased.

'You have no idea,' he grunted.

But I knew exactly how he felt, and I wanted him to *fuck* me. So I clenched my thighs, squeezing him inside me. His faltering moan made me grin against the stairs.

'*Amanda*,' he threatened.

So I did it again, clenching harder. One of his hands slid into my hair, pulling my head up until his mouth met my ear.

'You're begging for a load of hot cum, are you trying to get me to *breed* you?'

Thankfully, I was on the pill. But the idea of Henry pinning me down and filling me with his babies had my temperature soaring, not the reality of it, but the fantasy.

'I'm on the pill,' I whispered to assure him, before I clenched again and arched, grinding myself against him to take him even deeper. 'Breed me, Sir.'

'You are a little devil,' he said, wrapping one hand around my throat and pulling his hips back before slamming back into my. The wooden treads bit into my hips, the pain mingling with the sweet pleasure his cock unleashed within me. 'No wonder you need taming, nothing but filthy thoughts in that head of yours.'

'Yes,' I moaned as he thrust again, scooping his hips right when I thought he was as deep as he could go to gain even more friction.

'This.' *Thrust.* 'Cunt.' *Thrust.* 'Is.' *Thrust.* 'Mine.'

God, I wanted that to be true. To spend the rest of my days knowing this sweet man could look after me with so much care, but still pin me to the floor and threaten to breed me with his pierced cock in the next breath.

My limbs grew heavy as he fucked me, pleasure filling my body with pure heat. Pressure coiled between my thighs, my pussy starting to clench involuntarily. I all but cried when Henry pulled out of my completely.

'I need to see your face,' he demanded, turning me over so my ass was on a stair. He took his place between my thighs, and I watched rapt as he slid his cock back inside me, the metal disappearing along with the length. It was utterly salacious seeing him fill me, watching the way I flared around him as he pulled back. Wrapping one fist in my hair, he pinned himself against me, pressing his other hand between us to tease my clit.

Within seconds, I saw stars. Henry's thrusts grew more erratic, harder but less smooth, and he tipped my face to his.

'That's it, Amanda, you're taking me so well. Let's make that sweet cunt clench around me, and I'll give you every fucking drop.'

'Please,' I begged. 'I need it.'

'I know, baby. Just need to be filled morning, noon and night.'

I came with a force that stole my breath, wrapping my arms around Henry's shoulders and clinging on for dear life as he slowed his strokes, making them longer, deeper, harsher. I quaked beneath him, his mouth settling over my throat as I whimpered.

'Fuckkkk...' he growled, his muscles tensing beneath my touch as he filled me to bursting.

I kissed him until he slumped against me, both of us utterly spent.

In the silence of the grand stairwell, all I could hear was the dripping of his cum as it leaked from us, landing on the polished wood beneath.

I had never been undone like that in my life. Never been fucked so thoroughly, and I wasn't sure I ever wanted to be put back together without him.

twenty-eight

```
OTTERLEIGH BAY VILLAGE NEWS
Weather forecast: Overcast with
     a chance of thunder
```

HENRY

Morning found Amanda wrapped around me as the sun peeked in through my curtains. With no one to see to, we'd slept long.

Merv would be eager for breakfast, but I wanted just a little longer pressed up against my girl before heading out into the slushy garden. I'd also need to drop a bottle of the expensive champagne the clients had left with Lisa to thank her for watching my donkey-friend while I went home.

The sun crept in through the half-drawn curtains, dusting everything in pale gold. Sliding a dark tress from her face, I admired my sleeping beauty. So serene. You wouldn't suspect that the night before, we'd been playing fuck-chase through the halls, with her begging to be filled with cum.

Two weeks ago, you couldn't have convinced me that someone so utterly perfect, so witty, and charming and devilish could walk into my life and upend it so thoroughly. I wanted to keep her. To wrap her in my arms and make her smile every single minute of the day.

She lay curled against me, impossibly peaceful with one hand tucked beneath her cheek. It had been late by the time we fell asleep. After our rough first time together, powered by pure need, we'd lain in bed exploring each other at a more leisurely pace. Finding each other in a slowed, sweeter but no less satisfying way.

Her hair spilt over the pillow in a dark waterfall, mussed where I'd tugged and twisted it. A faint flush lingered across her cheeks, her lips still pink and swollen from endless kisses. And other uses of her pretty mouth.

Looking at her made me ache. How could I be in bed with her and yet yearn for her so thoroughly? It was like she still lingered in the temporary, the end of her time at Bayview Maor quickly approaching. She wasn't a fragile kind of beautiful. She was the type of beautiful you wanted to worship and tease, bite and kiss, pin and torment. The type that burrowed deep and left a lingering bitemark on your soul.

My finger brushed along her temple, dipping down over her jaw. She shifted, settling closer, seeking my warmth.

My chest tightened with a fierce tenderness I wasn't prepared for

Last night had been...

Christ.

There were no words for it.

She'd given herself to me in ways I'd only imagined in the quietest, most devious corners of my mind. She'd run from me, bit me, and finally surrender beneath me, taking pleasure like she was born for it. She'd trembled under my hands and whispered my name into the early hours, branding the night on my bones.

Was it a fling?

Fuck, no.

There existed no universe in which this woman was temporary. I couldn't fathom it.

I wanted to keep her.

To love her.

To take her home every year, and build our own

traditions. To build a life. Was it too fast? Maybe. But I no longer cared. How could you put a timescale on the feelings swelling in my chest?

I wanted her mornings and her evenings, to know her favourite things and her worst habits. I wanted her rolled eyes and bright laughter. I wanted to know every inch of the life she'd lived before she stepped into mine.

The weight of it hit me so swiftly that I leaned forward and pressed a kiss to her throat, right where her pulse beat beneath the skin.

She let out a small, sleepy noise that made my stomach clench.

Another kiss, along the curve of her chest.

Another, lower.

She stirred, eyelashes fluttering before she finally cracked one eye open, squinting at me with that half-conscious irritation she got when pulled from sleep.

'What are you doing?' she said huskily. 'Why are we waking up when we don't need to?

I grinned. 'Because I'm very bored without you.'

She made a sound that was somewhere between a groan and a laugh, burying her face in the pillow as I grinned like an idiot.

'So, serious question,' I said, wrapping an arm

around her waist and pulling her back flush to my chest. 'What's your favourite food?'

'What?'

'Favourite food,' I repeated, grazing my fingers over her hip. 'And your favourite colour. And an animal. And season. And book. And childhood toy. And smell. And—'

'Oh my God.' She tried pulling the blanket over her head. 'It's too early for twenty bloody questions.'

'No, it's not. I want to learn everything about you. Right now. I'm starting from the basics. Favourite food. Go.'

She blinked at me, an edge of amusement and horror in her eyes. 'You're so weird. '

'Thank you,' I said, leaning in to kiss her shoulder.

She groaned, then gave in and laughed. 'Pasta. Blue. Bears. Autumn. Kushiel's Dart. A stuffed penguin I cried over when my mum threw it out. And cinnamon.'

'Your mum threw your teddy out?'

'Mmhmm. When I turned twelve. Apparently, toys are for babies.'

'Well, you're my baby. I'll get you a toy.'

She rolled her eyes, exasperated. 'I have plenty of the type of toys *you'd* be interested in.'

'Filthy bitch,' I said, tugging her on top of me and kissing her.

'Takes one to know one,' she said against my lips.

The village hall shone like it was part of an M&S Christmas ad.

Half the village was already gathered inside, confused about the aisle between the usual tables that opened onto the dance floor.

Morag elbowed Isla, Owen's sister, so hard she nearly toppled over.

'Something's afoot,' she said, smug as anything. 'I told Alistair over breakfast. Have you ever seen the place decorated to the nines like this?'

Alistair nodded the way men do when they're not entirely sure what they're agreeing with. 'Aye. This is a lot for the ceilidh. We're usually lucky if we have a couple of strings of lights. I hope the committee hasn't footed the bill for this.'

'We'd need a lot of bake sales to cover it,' Morag added.

Eilidh, wrapped in possibly the sparkliest, pinkest

dress I'd ever seen, stood beside Amanda, on the other side of me. 'Why's the bar closed?'

Scruff trotted between everyone's shoes, wearing a tiny tartan bowtie and looking very pleased with himself. For once, Morag's dog was stickless. A rare occurrence.

Meanwhile, Meowrse, Owen's selectively favouritism-offering cat, had appeared on the edge of the stage, clearly not one to miss the festivities. Scruff passed him and growled, and with one look, Meowrse sent him packing.

The canopy of lights and foliage about had held up well overnight and, through the day, shimmered like a distant galaxy. Ivy and holly curled around the beams, a few sprigs of eucalyptus poking through the cedar. The lanterns cast a honey-warm glow over the wooden floor that had definitely seen more ceilidh dancing than weddings.

Jean stood in the corner bossing around three grown men.

'No, Kenny, not there. Honestly, if I left you alone for five minutes, this place would look like a jumble sale.'

The ceilidh band broke into a charming folk version of All You Need Is Love. Slightly odd with an accordion and a fiddle, but it did the job.

Amanda's hand found mine as the doors opened, and like magic, the humanist appeared from the side kitchen, taking her place on the dance floor.

Claire walked in on Owen's arm, her dress like something straight from the faerie glens. A deep sage green, covered in tiny amber blooms, with dramatic sheer sleeves.

Gasps and cheers filled the air. A noise from Jean that sounded akin to a ferociously boiling camp kettle.

Claire glowed, her red hair pulled into a loose braid, similarly studded with amber flowers, her cheeks flushed, eyes bright. Owen was beaming, proud as punch to be marrying his best friend. His soul mate. His kilt swished as he walked through the crowd, hands clapping his shoulders as he passed.

My chest tightened as I fought back a wave of emotion. For Jean, who had joined Jim and beamed at her son. For Owen and Claire, having pulled off their perfectly planned, yet unplanned, wedding. And with the knowing that I wanted that. With Amanda. Come hell or high water.

Scruff barked and chased after Claire's train until he was scooped up by Eilidh, who gently chastised him.

Meowrse watched from the stage like some epic

overlord. Looking ready to give his blessing to two of the few people he actually liked.

Amanda squeezed my fingers.

'This is perfect,' she whispered.

'You helped make it perfect.'

'You look damn fine in your kilt, by the way,' Amanda said under her breath. I swallowed down my laughter and nudged her.

The ceremony itself was peak Otterleigh.

Jean dabbed her eyes with a tissue that emerged from her sleeve. Jim passed over the rings with all the solemnity of a proud father who was holding back from joining his wife in tears.

Isla loudly whispered, *'Told you he'd cry,'* when Owen's voice wobbled.

Eilidh openly bawled into Scruff's fur.

When Claire and Owen finally kissed, the room exploded with noise. The fiddler launched into an enthusiastic tune as the rest of the band joined him with gusto. Scruff howled in celebration and then howled again because someone tried to shush him.

Meowrse took that as his cue to bugger off.

Then the ceilidh kicked off in style.

And sparkling, tartan-swirling chaos took over. I spun Amanda around the dance floor until we both grew sweaty and tired.

People spilt across the floor in happy mayhem. Kids darted between dancers, risking life and limb to alleviate boredom as the night wore on. Isla's husband spun too hard and careened into a table of tablets, sending sugary confectionery flying, much to the joy of the children.

Scruff zigzagged, collecting fallen napkins like they were and tearing them into tiny pieces below the tables.

And right in the middle of it, Amanda let me pull her close. She fitted against me so perfectly as we danced, her cheek against my jaw as we spun beneath the lights. Her laughter erupted bright and addictive, and I basked in every second of it.

While we swayed and spun, reeled and bobbed, my mind raced to find a way to convince her to stay. Or to take me with her.

As the night wore on, Claire and Owen danced together, their love so open and easy that it made me ache. My joy for them only increased, having had a sliver of what they'd found.

I wanted it too.

twenty-nine

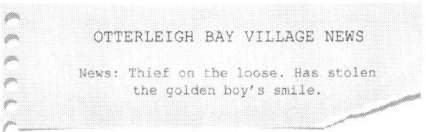

AMANDA

The morning felt heavy with the weight of what was to come.

The old manor creaked in the cold, but it was cosy in Henry's bed, wrapped in the circle of his body. Such a sweet place to be, but one I definitely didn't deserve.

Henry's arm was draped over my waist, where he'd fallen asleep when we finally got home from the ceilidh. His chest rose and fell against my back, each breath brushing me in a way that made my skin goosebumpy. Little echoes of last night's happiness.

The ceilidh.

The stolen kisses in dark corners as the clock struck midnight.

That look he gave me when I whispered 'Happy New Year'.

Like I'd accidentally offered him a forever.

It terrified me how easy it would be to just never go home. To hole up inside Bayview Manor, getting adored all day and railed to within an inch of my life all night. I could see why so many women lose themselves for premium cock.

Henry groaned when I shifted, needing to pack up my things if I was going to make my train.

'Don't,' he mumbled into my hair, voice thick with sleep. 'I'm not ready for you to start escaping.'

'I need to pack.'

He nosed gently at the back of my neck, and that small, domestic intimacy made my throat choke up. So many years of dreaming about having someone who wanted all of me just as I am. Only to find it in the worst place. Why couldn't Henry live in Edinburgh? A city romance I could do. Maybe. Even then, Henry deserved someone better than me. Someone who would flourish in a village where everyone knows everyone. Someone sunny, bright, and cheerful who could fill his house with cherubim.

'Stay,' he murmured. 'Just a bit longer.'

I rolled onto my back, and he shifted with me, draping himself half over me like a determined golden retriever who'd found his favourite toy and refused to give it up. His hair stood up in soft peaks, making him look sweet and sexy, and impossibly tempting.

Those blue eyes opened slowly, squinting at the pale January light leaking through the curtains.

'Morning,' he said.

'Hey.' I rolled over briefly, grabbing two mints and popping one in each of our mouths.

'Are you saying a stink, Princess?'

'No matter how hot you are, even you get morning breath after a night on the beer.'

'Terrible lies,' he groaned, 'But this must mean you want me to kiss you.'

'I do.'

'I'm taking that as a marriage declaration. Merv will back me up as a witness.'

'Merv isn't even in the room.' I giggled and snuggled into his chest.

'Can you prove that to whoever is in charge of weddings?'

Eventually, he pulled back and studied me for a long moment, and it hit me: he really saw me. Not the polished version I gave everyone else. Not the efficient, put-together Amanda I was so good at performing. But the full-on messy version.

And he looked like he liked what he saw.

Which was absurd.

'Otterleigh Bay's got plenty to offer, you know,' he said, his voice dipping into that coaxing tone he used when he was trying to win someone over. 'You don't need to run off to some sun-soaked beach to mend yourself. You could stay. With me.'

He stroked the inside of my wrist, sending affection roiling through me.

'There are pastries. And sunshine if we walk up to the headland early enough. And I'd very much like you to stay.'

My heart flipped, stupidly, the way it only ever did with him.

I looked away, because meeting his eyes would give me away.

He'd see that I wasn't right for him at all.

He deserved someone like Claire, warm and sweet, who fit in here.

Someone who wanted a village and a house full of children, and everyone up in their business.

Someone who wasn't me.

'I can't,' I said softly. 'I really can't. The Leadbetters will be back tomorrow, and I've already stretched my welcome. I've got work piling up, and flights to look at, and clients who'll need me and—'

'And what do *you* need?' he interrupted.

The truth was simple: Him.

But also complicated. I needed my career, and Uber. And the anonymity of the city. Someone who wanted to travel with me, and who only wanted one kid, far into the future.

'I don't know,' I admitted. 'Everything feels lovely here. Too lovely. It's been weddings and fairy lights and everyone high on romance. It's a new year, and I'm tired and sentimental, and it's too easy to be wooed by something that isn't reality.'

Something flickered in his face, and he tried to hide it, but I saw it before he could. Pain.

It felt like being stabbed with a shiv I'd fashioned myself.

'It *is* real. Maybe it's magic as well, but those aren't mutually exclusive.'

I closed my eyes. I couldn't look at him and say what came next.

'Maybe we shouldn't decide anything now. Maybe we... keep things open-ended. See what happens when we're back in our actual lives. Text, talk, whatever feels natural. No big declarations. No promises.'

He stilled.

Not angry, but quiet. Like he was assessing the gap I was hammering between us.

Panic crawled up my spine.

Then he exhaled and pressed his forehead against mine.

'Open-ended,' he repeated. His lips brushed mine. 'Alright. If that's what you want, I'll take it.'

'It's what's sensible,' I confirmed.

'Sensible,' he echoed. It sounded bitter in his mouth. After a long moment, he mustered a small, careful smile.

'I suppose I can try sensible. For now.'

A tear slipped down my cheek before I even realised it had escaped. I felt like I was making a mistake, but I needed some level of protection around me. I feared that as soon as we weren't holed up in the same building, any cracks would expand into gulfs, and I'd be the one who toppled in. Henry could have any woman he wanted at the drop of a hat.

Henry caught my tear with his thumb.

'But Amanda, just so you know... I'm not done obsessing over you.'

I didn't know whether I wanted to be the woman he wanted or the woman he needed. But I didn't believe that both were the same thing.

thirty

> OTTERLEIGH BAY VILLAGE NEWS
>
> News: Thief on the loose. Has stolen the golden boy's smile.

HENRY

The January wind sliced straight through my coat, my cheeks stinging. It was bollock freezing weather. Our breath ghosted in the air as we stood side-by-side on the platform. Amanda stood with her hands tucked into her pockets, her shoulders hunched against the cold, and her guard firmly back in place.

She kept staring down the track as if the train might appear and save her from the awkwardness of a goodbye.

I wanted to touch her. To steady her with a hand at her back. My thumb brushing over her jaw. Something to mark that last ten days we'd had weren't just a fling. But we had already dragged it all out at Bayview. Another kiss would have made it harder, not easier. So I kept my hands shoved deep in my coat pockets, nails curling into my palms.

'You'll text when you get there?' I asked, hating how unsure my voice sounded.

'Yeah, of course.' She offered a smile. It was far too polite, nothing like the ones she'd given me when she'd been wrapped around me in my bed. But her eyes gave her away. They gleamed in the afternoon light, showing the only emotion she couldn't control with sheer defiance.

Like she might be leaving more behind than she wanted too.

A low rumble through the rails announced her train's approach. She flinched and I felt like someone had torn my guts out through my arsehole.

'So,' she said, rocking slightly. 'This is…'

'Not the end,' I said quickly. *Too quickly*.

God, I was pathetic.

Pathetically in over my head for her. I couldn't make her stay, but I would convince her that a few hours between us wouldn't temper my ardour.

She breathed out a shaky laugh. 'Open-ended. Remember?'

'Right. Open-ended.'

When the train finally pulled in, she stepped forward with her bag, and all I could do was follow a pace behind, hands useless at my sides. She turned just before stepping on board, cheeks pink from the cold, hair whipping around her shoulders. I couldn't let her leave without a last kiss.

I stepped forward, grasping her to me and pressing my mouth to hers, tasting her sweet, minty breath on my tongue. Tugging her hair gently, I encouraged her to open up for me. She wavered in my arms, her breath coming in short pants as I poured everything into that one kiss. All my desire. All my awe for her. All my wants for the future.

She gave as good as I did, until people bustled past us, forcing me to let her go.

'Thanks for everything, Henry,' she said. And before I could ask what *everything* meant, she stepped onto the train. It took everything not to follow her.

'I'll see you,' she said. No soon. No promise.

'I'll see you *soon*,' I added, letting her know I'd be a little more dogged than she.

And then she was gone inside the carriage, finding a seat by the window. I stood on the platform like a bellend, waiting for her to look at me. She didn't.

The train hadn't even begun rolling when my phone buzzed.

I glanced down, expecting it to be the Leadbetters or one of my family.

Instead, it was Amanda.

> Thank you for showing me how good it can be to let go in safe hands.

Another ping.

> Thanks for being those safe hands, Henry.

Heat hit me all at once, squeezing the air from me as her train departed the station.

I replied.

> Hope "safe" isn't the only way you'll remember my hands, Princess.

I stared at the screen, the icy wind cutting around me. And I waited for her reply. And waited.

The manor was too quiet when I returned from the station, everything in the manor reminding me of

Amanda. I made a coffee out of habit more than desire, hands half-numb from the platform.

I took the mug outside, frost crunching beneath my boots as I headed for the stables. Merv poked his head out before I reached the door, ears pitched forward and nose snuffling for treats.

'Alright, mate,' I said, pressing him backwards and stepping inside.

He shuffled into me as I sat on an upturned bucket, trying to stop Merv from knocking my coffee out of my hand.

'Alright, alright. Calm down,' I said, abandoning my coffee and rubbing between his ears. His fur was warm under my palms, comforting in a way that only animals can bring with their lack of judgment.

I leaned against his side, letting my forehead rest briefly against his rising and lowering coat.

'I think she's the one,' I told him. The words escaped before I could second-guess them. 'I know it sounds mad. Too soon. Too rash. I really do.'

Merv snorted and kicked over my coffee.

'Yeah.' I stared into the middle distance. 'Trouble is... how do I make her see it? How do I make her see that it's not fake just because it's fast?'

I glanced down at my phone, pulling her

messages up on my screen. 'It's not over until it's over, right buddy?'

'Open-ended my arse.'

Outside, the wind whistled through the yard. Merv let out a low bray.

And for the first time since she'd stepped on that train, I stopped wallowing and decided to concoct a plan.

thirty-one

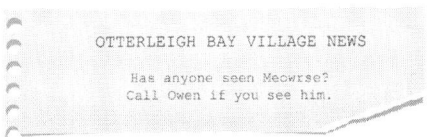

AMANDA

By the time the train rattled into Waverley, I was feeling all too sorry for myself. The city was washed in grey-white, the snow having turned to slush along the streets. Even the ground reminded me of Henry.

I dragged my bag along the short walk home. Every step felt heavier than the last.

Megan opened the flat door before I even got my key in.

'Bloody hell,' she said quietly, her eyes searching my face. 'Come here.'

I didn't ask how she knew that something was

wrong. She just did. She pulled me into her arms, and it took everything not to bawl right there on the doorstep. Her jumper was soft against my cheek and smelled like home.

Or what I'd always thought of as home. Which was her.

'Come on, you, let's get you on the floor.'

I made to object, but let her drag me to the sitting room, dumping off my wet books and coat on the way. She was already grabbing the Maltesers and pushing me to the floor. We ended up on the rug, just like we always used to, our backs on the floor and feet hooked up onto the cushions. The bag of malted chocolates lay between us.

Snow settled thick on the window ledge. The hiss of traffic snaking by outside.

Megan waited patiently. She never cajoled. It was both the worst and best thing about her.

'It's a boy,' I said with a sigh.

'Ah. It always is.' She nodded, as if that explained everything. Which it sort of did.

I pressed a Malteser to my lips but didn't eat it. 'Meg... I don't know what I'm doing.'

'You don't have to know. Just spill.'

So I tried.

'He's kind,' I said, staring up at the ceiling. 'In a

steady way. And he makes the most terrible jokes that shouldn't make me laugh, but they do. And he—'

My voice faltered until I swallowed. 'He looks at me like he can't believe I'm real.'

Megan shifted, looking sideways at me. But she didn't interrupt.

'And I felt like I belonged, not in the village, but in his arms. And I liked it. Too much. Which is a problem?'

'Is it?'

'Yes, because I know what happens when people rely on each other. Mum and Dad were in love until they weren't. They adored each other before they couldn't stand the sight of each other. It all went wrong so fast. And I don't want to wake up one day in that kind of misery.'

Megan rolled her eyes and threw a Malteaser at my head. 'You're not them, Amanda.'

'What if I am?'

'You're not.' She said with conviction. 'You're careful. And thoughtful. He clearly cares for you. And you're doubting your choices. What's the harm in giving it a try?'

'I couldn't stay. He asked. And God, Meg, I wanted to. I wanted to curl up right in his lap and let him make all the hard choices for me. But I panicked, because that's not who I want to be. I said we should keep it open-ended.'

'Do you want it open-ended?'

I closed my eyes. Sirens passed outside, throwing blue lights across the ceiling.

'No. I want... I don't know. I want everything he has to offer, but without losing who I am. And without getting hurt.'

Megan bumped her shoulder gently into mine. 'You'll miss all the good stuff when you spend your life avoiding the bad.'

Tears pricked at the corners of my eyes before I could stop them.

She pushed the Maltesers nearer. 'Here. Sugar solves at least half of all emotional breakdowns. And if it doesn't work, we'll try tea. And if that doesn't work, we'll move on to the wine.'

I laughed through my tears.

'Tell me what he's really like,' she said. 'Not the boring stuff. The bits you remember when you close your eyes.'

And just like that, the words came easier.

'He's warm,' I said. 'Like you. And he holds me like he's afraid I might vanish if he lets go even for a second. He's got this sleepy morning hair that makes him look like a corrupted angel, and when he smiles, it makes my insides turn to jelly.'

'You know, for someone who claims not to do romance, you really sound like someone falling in love.'

I groaned and covered my face with both hands.

'What else do you think about when you close your eyes?' Meg asked.

'Nothing that it's decent to tell my little sister.'

She rolled onto her side, eyes like saucers. 'Well, now I'm getting the wine, and I need you to spill the juicy stuff.'

I laughed and felt a thousand times lighter already.

thirty-two

> OTTERLEIGH BAY VILLAGE NEWS
> Never mind. Meowrse turned up with a
> lady cat, even more aloof than usual.

AMANDA

Two days passed, and every hour seemed to stretch full of too much space and not enough air. I kept pretending to Megan that I was fine, and absolutely not checking my phone every fifteen minutes, but she wasn't fooled. She kept handing me cups of tea like I was a dried-out houseplant. Who drank tea.

By the second evening, I gave up my resolve and picked up my phone.

I sat on the edge of my bed with my heart hammering in my chest. I stared at the blank message field for longer than I'd meant to, my most recent tea growing cold enough to gain a film.

> Hey.

> Would it be all right if I came down to visit for a couple of days?

> I know I was a bit vague before, but I'd like to try.

> With you.

> If you still want to.

The moment I hit send, sweat swept over my neck. I flopped onto my back, arms flung dramatically outwards like I was fifteen, not nearly double that. I felt as nervous as a teenager texting a boy for the first time.

My phone buzzed.

I bolted upright, heart in my throat.

> No.

Just that sole devastating word.

Cold.

Blunt.

Final.

It hit so hard I felt like someone had come in and stomped right on my chest, fuck. Had a bit of sense made him re-evaluate me?

My head went into a brain-blending meltdown. Had it only been sex? If so, Henry deserved a bloody Oscar. Had I been too needy? Did his family decide that he needed someone more fitting? Had I made it weird?

I ruined it. He'd changed his mind. Of course, he'd changed his mind, you absolute twat-faced bell end.

I was halfway into a full, catastrophic spiral when someone knocked at the front door.

A sharp, manly knock.

I froze. Megan appeared from the kitchen, eyebrows raised, and brandishing a wooden spoon like a weapon.

'You expecting someone?'

I shook my head. My legs felt detached from the rest of me as I followed Megan down the hallway. The knock came again, more insistent.

I opened the door.

And Henry stood there, a mop of blond curls whipped up by the wind.

He was dusted in snow, flakes caught in the mess of his hair. There was a bag slung over his shoulder, like he wasn't just making a pit stop.

'You can't visit.' His voice was low and a little breathless.

My brain hadn't caught up. 'What?'

He stepped closer, snow crunching beneath his boots.

'You can't visit *me*,' he repeated, 'because I'm not home.'

The words slid into place at once, my heart lurching.

He came to me.

Before I could form another thought, he dropped his bag and cupped my face in both hands. I didn't care an ounce that his fingers were ice cold. The touch was so familiar and so wanted, I all but melted the moment he touched me.

Then he kissed me.

It wasn't rushed or frantic; it was slow and certain, like he'd been craving the moment just as badly as me. I held onto the fabric of his snow-dusted coat lest I float away.

When he finally pulled back, his forehead pressed against mine, and we were both breathing as if we'd just finished a marathon.

I managed a whisper. 'How did you find me?'

He brushed his thumb along my cheek as if he couldn't help touching me. 'When you obsess enough over someone, there's always a way.'

My eyebrows creased, my heart was thudding so loudly I was sure he could hear it.

'Henry...'

He grinned, sheepish and proud all at once. 'Alright. Lady L had your Edinburgh address on one of your invoices. She told me not to misuse it. So I immediately disobeyed.'

'You drove all the way from Otterleigh Bay?'

Through snow and ice. And I'd do it all again for one god damned kiss. Although I'm really hoping you'll let me in.'

The pleasure that whisked through me had me tugging him inside. I'd spent so long pretending I didn't need anyone that I'd not seen the woods for the trees.

'Thank you.' I reached up and planted another slow kiss on him when I got him safely indoors.

Megan clapped beside me before squealing. 'You must be Henry. I've heard soooo much about you.'

'Megan,' I threatened.

'All good, I hope?' Henry said, giving my sister a sunny smile.

'Something about a little piece of metal...'

I picked up a brush and threw it at her.

But I didn't care.

Henry was here.

He'd chosen to be here.

And for the first time, trying didn't feel like a risk.

thirty-three

> OTTERLEIGH BAY VILLAGE NEWS
> Bon voyage to Henry, safe travels.
> The village committee has requested him back
> by spring. Someone needs to think of the roses.

HENRY

The Maldives' sun baked my skin, toasting me like an oversized Scottish marshmallow. It was late January, thirty degrees Celsius, with the sea stretching out as far as the eye could see. I still hadn't quite wrapped my head around the fact that I was there.

Half lying and half melted into a private sunbed with Amanda tucked against my chest, one leg thrown over mine as if she'd claimed me.

She was scribbling numbers into a Sudoku book with utmost focus, her nose crinkling as her eyes followed the rows and columns. It was like gobbledegook to me. Really, I was just enjoying the view of her in today's spectacularly small bikini.

'No, look,' she sighed, tapping her pen against a box. 'If the seven goes here, then the five has to be on this row, and the three can't go there—'

'Right,' I said, even though I didn't follow a damn thing, but I liked that she enjoyed it. She filled in the next three numbers with effortless precision.

I stared at the page, then at her, then back at the page. 'Is that it?'

'Sure is.' She took a sip of her cocktail before flopping back against me, basking like an upturned lizard.

'That took you all of about eight seconds.'

'It was an easy one to be fair.'

I love how smart you are. The brains to my brawn.'

She blushed, but tried to hide it by fiddling with the pen.

'It's just numbers. Is there anything else you adore?' she asked lightly, eyes flicking up, devilment waiting in those brown orbs.

'Oh, plenty.'

'Go on, then.'

'Alright...' I leaned back, letting the sun warm my chest. 'I adore the way your nostrils flare when you're being a complete control freak.'

She swatted my thigh. 'Charming.'

'And the way you soften when you finally stop overthinking and let me take care of things.'

She didn't swat me for that one. She just bit her lip and smiled.

I brushed my thumb along her waist. 'I adore how you love your sister. Fiercely. Without conditions and the way you show up for people, even when you think you're terrible at feelings.'

'I especially love the way you whimper and shake when I slide inside you, especially when I still and wait for you to squirm.'

She turned around in my lap until she was facing me, her knees on either side of my hips. 'Do you know what I love?'

'What?'

'You.'

My heart felt like it stopped, until she kick-started it with a deep kiss,

She loved me. Amanda *loved* me. Her admission had me utterly flabbergasted.

When she pulled back from the kiss, our breaths mingled.

'I love your hands. Your strong, rough hands and all the wonderful things you do with them.'

Her fingers slid down my forearm, tracing the veins there that she adored so much.

'I love how wild you are about Merv, even though he's a menace. I love that entire villages adore you and rely on you. It's how I knew you were a good man. The right kind of man. Even when you spank me and tell me you're going to put babies all up in my womb.'

My chest tightened. Hard.

She lifted one curl at my temple and twirled it. 'I love this too. These sweet blonde curls mask what a demon you are behind closed doors. This is why people don't know you're trouble.'

'I'm only trouble for you.'

'Luckily,' she teased, 'I enjoy trouble.'

I rested my hands on her hips, grounding myself so I didn't lose myself in sheer happiness. Her admission still ricocheting through my chest.

'How do we make this work when we go home?'

There it was, the question we'd been avoiding for days. The elephant lurking behind every kiss, every cocktail, every sleepy morning in the insanely soft bed here.

'Well,' I said, leaning in and dragging my lips over her exposed throat. 'I can come to Edinburgh on weekends. Lisa next door is always happy to help with Merv.'

Amanda nodded, a tiny moan escaping as I grazed my teeth over her collarbone.

'And maybe in between jobs, you could come up to Otterleigh Bay. See it when it's not half-frozen. When the wildflowers are out, and the bakery queue lasts thirty minutes because tourists lose their minds over Eilidh's buns. The Leadbetters are quite happy to have you there for sleepovers.'

I ran my fingers up her spine, adjusting her position in my lap until her eyes sparkled and her hips arched.

'We can make it work if we both want it.'

Amanda exhaled, her breath trembling ever so lightly.

'And what makes you think it will work?' She asked.

'Because I love you, baby. And that's all I need to follow you to the ends of the god damned earth.'

The sudoku book slid off the sunbed and landed in the sand as she pulled my lips to hers.

epilogue

HENRY

Leaves scratched across the cobbles as Amanda and I made our way through the village hand in hand, still a bit sleepy, and wrapped up in scarves and coats. Autumn had officially arrived.

Eilidh's bakery was toasty warm when we stepped inside, and the smell of cinnamon, butter, and strong coffee beckoned us in further.

'Morning, you two. You're up early.' Eilidh was busy transferring the fattest pumpkin cinnamon buns I'd ever seen onto a tray.

We spent the morning there, chatting with any

villagers or tourists who stopped by. Cuddling babies and petting dogs, drinking copious amounts of coffee and giggling with each other until our sides hurt. Even after the best part of nine months, I still couldn't drag my eyes from Amanda for very long. I was so helplessly in love with her that it pained me at times.

So I watched her blossom amongst my friends and family, finally realising that people liked her. Not for her successful job, or her smart clothes, but for her tenacious spirit and her open heart.

After breakfast, we strolled along the beach, chatting and mucking around. The air was filled with sea salt and the faint pong of seaweed, and I took her by the hand, walking until we turned a corner near the bluff below Bayview Manor.

And there on the sandy dunes stood Lisa.

And Merv.

The donkey was covered in flowers. A garland of dethorned roses around his thick neck, and wildflowers braided into his mane. He looked a little more ridiculous than I'd planned.

Amanda doubled over laughing. 'Oh my God, Henry, what have you done to Merv?'

Lisa waved cheerfully. 'He tried to eat half of it, but most of it survived!'

And then Amanda saw the ring hanging from the flower garland, tied neatly with twine.

My already burgeoning nerves broke free, making my fingers tremble as I gathered Amanda's hand.

Merv lumbered forward, his hooves sinking into the sand, ears pricking as he approached. Amanda's eyes shone as she covered her mouth, looking from Merv to me.

My heart beat so loudly in my chest that I worried she wouldn't hear me. I sank to my knees and looked up into her perfect face.

'Amanda, you've made every part of my life better just by being in it. I don't care where we live, or where we work, or how complicated everything gets. I want to promise myself to you for eternity.'

She laughed tearfully. 'I'm only asking for Edinburgh, not Antarctica.'

'That will make logistics easier, but if you decide to shack up with the penguins, count me in. Amanda, will you marry me?'

'Yes,' she said without hesitation. 'You're all mine.'

I grinned like an idiot and got to my feet, ready to untie the ring from my friend Merv. But Merv had other ideas. The fucker bolted full speed across the sand. Flowers flying behind him like he needed to leave breadcrumbs to find his way back. The ring bounced wildly against his chest.

'Merv!' Lisa shrieked, tearing after him.

'This wasn't the plan, you wee beast.' I joined the chase.

Amanda burst into helpless laughter and ran after us, sand kicking up behind her. Merv had a blast, dodging the three of us as we yelled and laughed.

Suddenly, Scruff appeared behind Amanda, with a stick roughly the length of a canoe balanced proudly in his mouth and charged across our path like a tiny saboteur.

Amanda had no chance.

She was swept right off her feet, landing in an undignified puff of sand.

I skidded to a stop and dropped beside her. 'Are you okay?'

She was cracking up, her hair wild and coated with sand. Tears at her lashes like tiny diamonds from the sheer chaotic madness of it all.

'Save the ring!'

With renewed vigour, I chased down the pesky ass until Lisa found an apple in the bottom of her nearby bag and used it to seduce our four-legged gannet. Relieving Merv of the ring, I went back to my girl.

She was still giggling and lay in the sand when I took her hand.

'Let's try this again.'

The ring slid perfectly onto her finger, as though it was always supposed to be there.

She pulled me down into the sand and kissed me until I began to see stars behind my eyes.

She was mine. And I was hers.

Forever.

AMANDA

My latest event landed me in the most adorable cottage in Glencoe. Surrounded by devilishly beautiful hills and forests, turning all the deep reds and oranges of autumn. I'd spent the best part of two weeks escorting a group of American business people around Scotland, going from Edinburgh to Glasgow, Stirling to a few of the islands, and finally landing near Mount Etive.

The clients were in a stunning seventeenth-century castle, and I'd been placed in one of the estate cottages. Not that I was complaining in the slightest. It meant that Henry had come up the previous night and would stay until the early hours on Monday.

Even better, the cottage bathroom held a claw-footed bath, and beyond it, a massive mirror.

I'd teased Henry for two days with pictures and videos of me in that mirror, in a myriad of outfits. And no outfit at all.

We'd been in too much of a rush to worry much about the bedroom when he'd arrived the day before, hell, we hadn't made it very far past the front door if I was honest.

There was little I enjoyed more than using our time apart to wind him up. Having your fiancé stride through the door and pin you to a wall in sheer desperation was quite the rush.

And although I regularly ceded control, I still very much enjoyed using my skills for leverage. Henry may be dominant in the bedroom, but he was still a man.

And now he had me sitting in his lap, facing the mirror, both of us stark naked. The lamplight lit us up from the side, a soft orange glow adding to the autumnal vibe.

'I missed you this week,' Henry crooned against my neck.

'You say that every week.' I whimpered as his

fingers stroked their way up my stomach, circling one breast before cupping the other.

'And it gets worse every time we're apart.'

While he pouted about missing me, he encouraged my work, always helping me to find fun new things for my clients to do, no matter which country I ended up in.

Henry's cock bobbed against my spread heat, that perfect metal ring visible in the mirror. I think taunting me with his hearness before letting me have it was one of his favourite games, and I couldn't deny how bloody needy it made me.

'Look at you, my darling. So fucking sweet.' Henry stroked his fingers over my hips before reaching around me and grasping his dick.

I watched hungrily as he reached around me, stroking himself with long pulls. It didn't take long before I was desperate to take his hand's place.

'Touch yourself for me,' he demanded, his gaze following my every movement in our reflection. 'Show me how badly you want it.'

'You know I want it,' I wheedled.

'Prove it. Spread that pretty cunt for your Sir.'

I obeyed, feeling my cheeks heating after all those months of our dirty, sexy games. My fingers slid between my thighs, spreading myself for his pleasure.

'Look how fucking wet you are,' he growled, his teeth catching my shoulder.

I let myself lean back against him as I touched myself, working my fingers over my clit as he reached up and taunted my nipples, pinching them until they peaked, all pink and angry. All that delicious pinching had me losing myself to pleasure, so close...

He kissed my shoulder. My jaw. Anything he could reach. Then he slid his dick inside me, not all the way, but angling himself so he hit the front wall of my vagina with every stroke. Pressure built quickly, until I squirmed in his lap.

'I'm want to fuck your ass, Princess. I think it's time. I want to see you watch me sink into you and coat that one part of you I've yet to claim.'

Nerves met lust as I worried my lip. We'd spent quite a few weeks working up to this. And every time I'd been left begging Henry to give me his cock, but as was his way, he'd made me wait.

He sank himself fully into my wet heat, grinding there until he had me right as the edge again, at which point he pinned my hands high and pulled that glorious, soaked, metal-topped dick out of me.

'Henry,' I cried. 'Give it back.'

He waited until my near orgasm subsided before repeating the process, taking me closer and closer to the edge each time. By the end of his fourth time, I would have taken the massive fucking mirror up my arse if it meant I could come.

'Ask for a good, hard ass-fucking, baby.'

'Please? I need to come.'

'Shall I paint your insides, my love?'

'Yes,' I moaned.

Henry steadied me while he rummaged in his bag, producing a bottle of lube and thoroughly wetting his cock down. Not that it hadn't already been dripping.

Then he altered my position, grasping me below each knee and lining himself up with my rear entrance.

'If you need to stop, tell me,' he demanded.

'I will.'

The tip pressed against me, and I watched rapt in the mirror at the absolutely hedonistic view we shared. He moved so slowly, sinking just the very tip into me. Breathing through my nose, I adjusted to the alien sensation. It felt so different to his fingers. Or his tongue. More intense. More painful. And altogether much filthier.

After a few moments, he sank further, his eyes rolling back as my body swallowed him up.

'Fuck,' he moaned, 'I'm never going to tire of the way this feels.'

The intense stretch stole my breath, but the sight of us in the mirror had me mesmerised.

'Henry.' My words came in a throaty whisper.

'Hold this leg up.' Henry instructed, and I obeyed, holding my left leg while he held my right. With his right hand, he reached between my legs and splayed me wide. From my soaked pussy right up to my sparkling engagement ring, there wasn't a single iota of me that didn't ache for him. To think I'd ever doubted us sounded crazy to me.

Imagine not having Henry there to bring me ice cream when I'm hormonal, or to bring flowers to brighten my flat. To miss out on the way he builds me up when I'm down and fucks me senseless when I need it.

I loved his cheeky smile and his wicked bite, his rough fingers and his pierced cock. His sweetness and sharpness collide with mine, balancing us both.

'Eyes on me,' Henry demanded, and I snapped my gaze back to his in the mirror. He slid two fingers into my waiting wetness, increasing the pressure building in my core. With a roll of his hips, his dick pressed deeper into my ass, and I whimpered.

'You can take it, baby. Or are you sad that I'm wasting my cum when I could be breeding you? You love it when I fill you with hot cum, don't you?'

'Yes, Sir.' I really did. As long as I had my pill.

Henry's breath quickened against my neck as he rocked inside my ass while curling his fingers, the two sensations driving me quickly to the edge. I just needed my fingers on my clit to tip me over.

'Can I touch myself?' I begged.

'No,' he growled. I writhed in his lap, being held on the precipice of blinding pleasure, had my muscles tense, my nerves sparking from head to toe.

'Please… Oh my god.' My thighs trembled as he quickened his pace, slamming his hips upward as I bounced in his lap. The view of us was downright pornographic.

'Not yet, baby.' He bit down on my neck, his teeth sending a sharp wave of acute pleasure roiling through me.

Sweat trickled between my breasts as he filled me, until I saw his balls tense in the mirror, drawing upward. I knew that moment well.

Henry's fingers circled my swollen clit, and it was like an electric shock. A wave of pleasure crashed over me, my muscles twitching uncontrollably as he pinned me to him, stroking me until I saw fireworks, ropes of heat coating my guts.

Well, damn. If he wasn't already marrying me, I'd be proposing to him myself.

afterword

Thank you so much for stepping into the Dom Next Door Series and Otterleigh Bay with our second couple, Henry and Amanda.

If you enjoyed The Grump Next Door, I'd appreciate a review wherever you usually leave them, but especially on Amazon.

You can find me on Instagram under Effie Raye Author.

A huge thank you to my family, who have supported me generously with time and understanding in bringing this book to life. Particularly, my darling

AFTERWORD

husband, having a partner who's a chaos gremlin with a deadline, is no feat for the weak.

Printed in Dunstable, United Kingdom